If hate is a game, this special ops man and ATF agent are out for blood. Or maybe they're just fighting to see who will be on TOP.

Special Ops Sergeant Lincoln Reed, aka Linc, doesn't want to talk about how small, dark places make him want to blow shit up. He wants to forget about that time of his life and get back to his team. But now he's trapped in an elevator with the annoying—and strangely pretty—ATF agent he's spent weeks trying to get off his back. She's a know-it-all on a power trip... and has he mentioned she's pretty?

One minute Nealy finds herself in a defunct elevator with a volatile special ops man and the next she's in his arms... with her naked thighs wrapped around him. Now she's forced to work even closer with him and the Ranger Ops team. She can't think of anything worse than a bunch of chest-thumping gun-toting tough guys taking credit for her bringing down the biggest illegal weapons smuggler the US has seen in decades.

As their investigation takes them through two states and across the Mexican border, Linc and Nealy are forced into an even tighter situation and have no choice but to see it through till the end. But she's still a know-it-all, even if she can kiss the lips right off him. And she could do without the soft spot growing inside her for the man who's all mouth and muscles. Can she close the door on this case *and* keep her heart intact?

Ranger Ops

Point Blank Range

by

Em Petrova

Chapter One

Linc's face bounced off something rough—ground. He could taste the dirt, and it definitely wasn't Texas soil. He'd tasted enough of that as a kid playing with his twin brother.

Lennon would get him out of this jam. Linc wasn't panicking—yet.

His mind blanked on the events that had gotten him here. The woods and explosions, his special ops team on the winning end of a fight. Then an arm like a vise around his throat, being dragged over logs and roots and finally knocked over the head.

He'd come to in the back of a truck surrounded by blackness and the acrid stench of pig shit. It had taken him seconds to realize the bastards were smuggling weapons in feces and since nobody wanted to dig around in the manure and inspect the cargo, they rolled across the border with AR-15s, AK-47s and enough semi-automatic pistols to put into the hands of half the children in schools across the United States.

Dammit, he and the Ranger Ops, with the help of Knight Ops had been *this* close to stopping it. They still could, but Linc was out of the game right now.

He was not helpless, though. He pretended to be unconscious while his mind was extremely alert, gathering everything about his surroundings and the people who had captured him.

They stopped dragging him, leaving him lying on his side, curled forward. It did not help him prevent the sharp kick to his gut. He wheezed and coughed as all the burritos he'd eaten before the mission threatened to come back to haunt him.

"Open your eyes!" they demanded in Spanish.

Linc did so, digging deep to find his capture training he'd had early on in his career. First the Marines and a stint as Texas State Trooper, followed by the Texas Rangers. Man, all that seemed like a fluffy pillow of a life compared to Ranger Ops.

But he was part of Homeland Security now, a division called OFFSUS, and they had the best of the best protecting their country.

Pride and patriotism blocked out any pain resonating through his gut or his bruised face.

"Sit up!" he was ordered.

Linc's hands and feet were bound, and a rope encircled his neck like a dog on a leash. Using his abs, he crunched into a sitting position and stared at the men surrounding him. He cut off his reaction to them before it got him into deeper trouble. He'd been trained to submit while remaining in complete control.

Exaggerate your injuries.

Linc started coughing, hard enough to begin gagging. Then he leaned to the side and puked up what was left of his Mexican food. The men scattered out of his way, cursing at him. But after he was finished, one guy grabbed the rope around his neck and dragged him several feet away from the mess.

The smell still rose up, along with whatever pig shit remained on his clothes, making his captors wrinkle their noses. One fished out a cloth and pressed it to his face.

"*Agua,*" Linc said in a roughened tone.

"Get him some water," someone demanded. A second later, a bottle of water was pressed to his lips. He slurped quickly, mentally measuring the distance between him and the man holding the bottle. Gauging whether or not he could fight with all his limbs bound and a rope at the ready to string him up from the closest rafter.

He couldn't make his move yet.

After the man pulled the bottle from his lips, he raised his eyes enough to stare at the guy's chest. Then a bit higher to his throat, where a blotchy black tattoo covered one side. Not one of those sexy tattoos like the woman Linc had taken to bed a few months before, a spattering of flowers and delicate letters of some Latin poem. Linc couldn't recall the meaning of the words anymore — but he did remember how sweet she'd felt sinking over his cock.

"Name and rank," a captor demanded. There were three, each uglier than the last, with scars on their faces that Linc wanted to add to.

He *would* add to, as soon as he played the sympathy card enough to get his hands or feet unbound. Maybe both.

He held up his hands and winced, twisting against the binding.

"Stop that!" someone grated out in Spanish.

Linc ceased but gave him a pitiful look. "It's digging into my skin and I think my wrist is broken from being dragged."

"Name and rank!"

Realizing he must play nice and share his toys, he responded. "Lincoln Reed, Texas Ranger."

It wasn't totally a lie—he hadn't been officially cut from the roster. Which was good, because if OFFSUS decided to slash Ranger Ops, as they'd been threatening to for months, he would need a job.

"Do you want more water, Lincoln?"

He didn't respond. *Never say yes to any question.*

Staring at his bonds, his mind worked over several possible scenarios. Get close enough to trip one, steal his knife and cut his hands free before the other two jumped him. He'd have seconds at best— odds he wasn't ready to gamble on quite yet. He'd bide his time.

Where the fuck was his team? They had to know his whereabouts. Surely, he still held some device to

4

trace his location, unless his captors had stripped it all from him those precious seconds when he'd been unconscious and tossed into the truck.

He was somewhere in Mexico, by his guess. The building was remote, with no sounds of city or cars. There weren't any windows to escape from or even tell the time of day.

Keep your shit together. You have the upper hand. You always will.

He had just enough cockiness to see him through, and he was damn happy he'd ignored his momma when she'd told him to be humble all those years.

Trying again, he held up his bound hands, keeping his head bowed as if too exhausted to even beg anymore.

"We can't cut you free, Lincoln. Now tell us who you are with. Who sent you to the forest to attack our men?"

With eyes trained on the dirty cement floor, he did not respond.

"We took this off you."

He glanced up. Fuck—it was his Blackhawk, a brand new high-tech gadget that Ranger Ops had just been given. Barely tested and not known to the general population but essential for special forces.

"This looks to be special forces, Lincoln. Are you in special forces?"

He did not respond, only hung his head. His seconds left to attack were ticking away, but he

5

needed the other two men of the group to spread out, giving him enough time to fight back before they jumped him.

Lennon, if you're out there, get the fuck here — now.

He and his twin had rarely had moments of the telepathy some boasted, but if ever he needed that link, it was now. He concentrated on his brother and next his other brothers — the ones he'd spilled blood with and fought beside for months now, his Ranger Ops brothers.

Nash, Shaw, Jess, Cav... they had to be searching for him. Hell, the Knight Ops team would be on it too. They wouldn't just let one of theirs go missing.

"Answer me! Are you special forces?"

When he did not respond, two men rushed forward and grabbed him. Yanking him to stand and holding him up, as he didn't have any stability with his feet bound so close together. The rope tightened around his neck, and he was shoved against a wall. He tasted blood as his face smashed into wood, but he bit back the pain, compartmentalizing it into a space deep inside himself, where nobody could touch him. A place he did not want to test the depths but would if he had to.

He drew a breath through his nose. It was bleeding as well.

"We know you're special forces, Lincoln." The man's voice projected into his ear.

"Why did you bother to ask?" he shot back.

The blow to the head took him down. He crumpled. They held him up as lights flashed behind his eyes. He fought against the black tunnel barreling his direction. If he was knocked out, he couldn't fight, couldn't gather intel, couldn't survive.

He needed his wits.

But it was too late—his vision closed in.

* * * * *

Maybe three days later

Linc crouched in a position his captors had forced him into in an attempt to break him, with his back against a wall and his legs forced out in front of him so his gluts and quads burned.

Little did they know, but they were up against a wall-sit champion. In gym class, he and his twin would compete and crouch in this same pose for half an hour at a time without batting an eye and only throwing occasional grins at each other.

But Linc was beginning to cramp. After days of no food and little water, he was in a weakened state, and his hopes were quickly draining.

He had gone from thinking *what can I do to get out of this* to *I might not ever get out of this.*

The interrogation went on and on, with his captors demanding information on how many forces were after them, what US intelligence knew about their locations and so on. He remained silent and had some cracked ribs and a busted nose for his trouble.

They yanked him upright, and his screaming leg muscles flexed with relief. He hung forward, panting and grateful in a way that made him want to bellow in rage. He would not give up, would not give in. No fucking way would these bastards take him out before his time.

Then they locked him in the crate.

* * * * *

One day later

Okay, he was losing it now. How many hours had he been in this black box? The walls closing in on him like a fucking coffin. He might as well be buried alive—he had just as much chance of getting out.

His brothers weren't coming for him. He'd never see his twin's face again, or his momma either. She'd worked two jobs to keep food in their bellies and a roof over their heads after their daddy split, and now Linc would never be given the chance to hug her again and thank her for all her sacrifices.

The walls were too close, smashing him into a shape that was no longer human. The walls of his mind were collapsing too, and that scared Linc more than anything.

He could not—would not—give away a single hint of information to these motherfucking captors. He had to survive.

At least he was no longer bound. With the crate as an effective jail cell, he wasn't a threat, and he was free to roam in the prison of his shipping crate. Metal walls no longer than eight foot square. He could lie down, but sleep didn't come easy. Night terrors—day terrors—he couldn't get more than a few minutes of sleep at a time before he'd wake with a scream on his tongue.

Yeah, he was fucking losing it.

He gave a short laugh.

Someone pounded on the metal, and he clapped his hands over his ears. This was another of their tactics to get him to talk—the pounding would go on for hours until he thought he'd lose his mind. Hell, he might have already lost it.

He laughed again, and this time one side of the crate opened, and something hard and plastic hit him.

A water bottle. He'd pissed in one corner several times now out of sheer necessity, but survival came first, and that meant he needed water.

He took the bottle and asked for a box to use as a toilet. The man's face was not visible—it was too dark. The man said nothing. The side was shut up again, and Linc was left alone.

He cracked the water open and had just brought it to his lips when the side of the crate opened again.

Something wooden scraped along the metal floor and then it smashed closed again.

The pounding started, but Linc abandoned the water and shut out the sound as he crawled on his hands and knees to examine what they had put in here with him.

In the blackness, it was difficult to determine what it was. A wooden box of sorts. He felt along the edges. One foot long by a foot wide, definitely wood. Tentatively, he reached in, expecting something to snap around his hand like the teeth of an animal trap.

He felt only bulky shapes.

What the fuck had they given him? *If only it was gunpowder, I'd blow myself outta here*, he thought.

Using caution, he withdrew an item from the box. Feeling the sides, top and bottom of the object, he couldn't make out what it was. He felt like he was playing that old game in Boy Scouts again, where you reach into a bag of rocks and feathers and other things and have to determine what it was you were feeling.

For countless minutes, he examined each object using only his sense of touch. A lumpy bag rattled too. The other objects didn't make a noise.

He ripped open the bag and tiny pebble-like items fell into his palm. He brought them to his nose and sniffed.

His stomach twisted as the cloyingly sweet scent of dried fruit hit him. He brought one to his lips and licked it. The sweetness made his empty stomach cramp.

They'd finally given him food. A care package.

Or the guy had just grabbed the nearest box without looking at the contents.

Linc couldn't eat much at once, or he'd be ill. He had to control himself and have a few at a time. Besides, who knew how long he would be stuck in this prison. This could be his last supper.

Linc popped one into his mouth and chewed. What were they? Dates? Raisins? The flavor nearly made him weep, and he blinked into the darkness to keep from letting the tears fall. After only five or six, he stopped himself and pushed the bag aside.

Then he found one canister had a lid. He opened it with a prayer on his lips that whatever it was wouldn't blow his ass to smithereens. When he dipped a finger into the contents, though, he found it oily. What the hell was it?

His lucid mind took note of his hysterical counterpart. *It's nacho cheese. You can make snacks for your guests.*

He sucked on his finger.

It wasn't cheese but lard.

What the fuck? He had a bag of dried fruit and some lard? The other container held something powdery, and upon tasting it, he realized it was flour.

A booming laugh escaped him. The assholes had given him a box of baking ingredients. Someone's

11

mother would be quite unhappy she never received the items on her grocery list and instead, the baking goods were locked inside a crate with an American prisoner.

He laughed again, and the pounding took over. It jarred his eardrums, his nerves, his mind until it threatened to unhinge him. But he pushed through the pain of the torture and opened the last container. This too was powdery.

But sweet.

Powdered sugar.

Linc's mind laser-focused on the items, and in seconds he had formulated a plan to get the fuck out of this crate.

He just needed a source of flame. He crossed his legs and leaned against the wall, popping the fruits slowly into his mouth as he bided his time.

Chapter Two

Linc's body was on fire. His skin melting. But he was slung over someone's bulky shoulder and they were running.

His head bobbed, and he was helpless to stop it. When the steps slowed, he heard the most beautiful sound in his life.

"Get him down. Help me get him down. He's fucking burned to a crisp." Shaw—his teammate, his brother in arms.

They had him.

Linc had gotten himself out of that goddamn crate. Fucked himself up in the process, but he'd done it.

Shaw's eyes loomed in front of his. "Hold on, man. We got you now. Waiting for airlift. Jesus Christ, who did this to you?"

He managed to lift a hand and tap his own chest.

"You did it?" Nash Sullivan's voice, on his nine. He swung his head toward the sound of his captain's voice and nearly cried with relief. They really did have him—this was not one of his nightmares of the past few days. He was out of that hell, and he would survive.

"They gave me baking supplies." A hysterical laugh bubbled from him, but it jolted his broken ribs and he wheezed in a breath. Fuck, that hurt too. *Lungs burnt – the explosion…* he thought distantly.

"He doesn't know what he's saying. I hear the chopper. Get him up, we'll run to meet it."

They lifted him again, this time in a two-man carry. Linc's skin was no longer on his body— couldn't be. It hurt like nothing else he'd ever experienced.

The sweet welcome of the chopper blades met his ears, and he was loaded onto transport.

Someone gripped his hand. He looked up at Shaw, the man's face etched with lines of concern and enough face paint to render him black.

"I'm out," Linc grated through dry lips.

"You are. Don't talk if it hurts. Do you know the extent of your injuries?"

He shook his head. "Ribs and nose broke. My legs—"

"Don't talk," Shaw said in a tight way.

He traveled the rest of the distance in silence, moving in and out of consciousness. This time his dreams were not haunted, but the agony in his legs kept him from truly resting. When he came to, he looked at his captain and said, "I ate all the fruit. I was too hungry."

"It's okay, man. We got you. Not long now."

14

He drifted again. Soon lights blared in his eyes, and he realized he was in the light of day.

"Jesus Christ." Shaw was staring at him.

"Don't look at it. He'll be okay. Get him in the vehicle." Nash lifted Linc.

"Someone thought he was being funny, giving a prisoner baking supplies. What was I gonna do with it—whip up a batch of cookies?" Linc said.

Both men stared at him as if he'd lost his mind.

He probably fucking had. They were dropping him off at the nearest nuthouse.

Linc laughed, and it hurt his ribs but he couldn't stop the joy that he had bested those motherfuckers.

"I cooked up something good. And I pickpocketed a lighter from one of those fuckers who held me prisoner in the crate."

"Fucking hell," Shaw said quietly.

Linc went on. "I lit the powdered sugar and heated the oil. When it had boiled a while, I threw the water on it and..." He spread his arms, though it hurt like hell, and created a cloud in the air to show the explosion.

It had gotten him out of the crate, and he'd crawled on his burned legs until he stopped feeling the pain. Then he'd gotten out of that place. He couldn't quite remember how Shaw and Nash had discovered him.

"How did you find me?" he asked in a gritty voice. "Can I have some water?"

They exchanged looks.

"If he needs surgery, he can't drink," Shaw said.

"Give him the goddamn water," Nash ordered.

"We stumbled over you in the fucking dark," Shaw said as Nash tipped water over Linc's parched lips. "Now lie back and rest. We need you whole, man."

He held up his hand again, and this time each of his teammates gripped it. "Guts 'n glory."

"Jesus. Do you ever stop being a hero, Linc?" Shaw's amused tone brought a smile to his face—this time it wasn't crazed.

* * * * *

This was it—the day Nealy had been waiting for. She clasped her hands in front of herself and waited for the announcement that she was being promoted to the position she had fought her entire career for.

The Acting Deputy Director of the ATF, the Bureau of Alcohol, Tobacco, Firearms and Explosives, had been in her sights for over a year now, ever since the announcement the former director would be stepping down soon to care for his ill wife. Since then, Nealy had amped up her game and laid herself on the line time and again in order to be seen.

She drew a deep breath. What if she wasn't promoted?

Nonsense—she was the most qualified here. She'd begun as an ATF agent in Miami, dealing with

16

drug and arms trafficking, with a resume under her belt that put her on the radar, and that had led her to management positions in the New York field division.

How many ladder rungs had she hoisted herself up to get to this day? She was more than prepared.

Hell, she had the white wine already chilling in her fridge back in her apartment.

She waited as the chief of staff closed out his talk and got down to the real business of appointing her.

Next to her, Mark Mitchum shifted in his chair. He was sweating slightly, a bead at his prematurely graying temple. Nealy's only competition in this game was Mark, but he wasn't nearly as qualified as she was, and she was confident in herself.

Here it was—Chief of Staff Holden was finally getting to the nitty gritty.

"Our new Acting Deputy Director will need to fill some big shoes. We will miss you, Bill."

A round of applause for Bill, who was looking somewhat relieved to be on his way down the ladder she was trying so hard to climb. No wonder, with his poor wife enduring chemo treatments.

"Now if you'll give a hand to Acting Deputy Director... Mark Mitchum!"

Nealy had scooted to the edge of her seat in order to stand for the acceptance, but the name of her coworker hit her like a two-by-four to the skull. She blinked at Mark's back as he stood to move forward and shake hands with Holden. Everyone was on their feet, applauding his success.

Mark's success, not hers.

Nealy bit down on her emotions, stood and clapped for Mark. She would allow the true disappointment and anger to take over later, when she could be alone with her wine. Right now, she must be poised and professional.

Mark looked right at her and sent her a wink.

Douche-bag. He had been giving her the whole little-sister act since she'd stepped foot in the DC office, but she didn't like the guy overall. He was the same age she was but condescending in the most subtle of ways that flew under any radars except hers.

Now he was her boss. What a shit-show.

As soon as the applause broke off, people moved forward to shake Mark's hand, sucking up to him, but Nealy rounded the outer edge of the group and found Holden.

"Sir, if I could have a word."

He eyed her. "I figured you'd be approaching me, Alexander. Follow me to my office, and we can get this over with."

That didn't bode well, but she allowed him to lead the way. When she closed the door behind them, the chief went straight to his desk and sank to the big chair. She stood before the desk, hands folded.

"Speak your peace, Alexander. I know you wanted that promotion."

No point in denying it. She nodded. "I did, sir. And I'd like to ask some questions, if you don't mind."

He waved to a seat, and she sank into it, gathering her thoughts.

"I wondered what actions I can take to be more qualified for the promotion next time. How do I stack up against these guys? How are my people skills in comparison?"

The chief looked impressed—and she did a mental victory dance that at least she was being taken seriously and wasn't coming off as a sore loser.

They spoke for a half hour, with him giving her good insights as to her own abilities and how to improve. Finally, he pushed a file across the desk to her.

"What is this, sir?"

"Your next case. A big one. I think you've heard of Operation X."

Her heart gave a little trip at the name dubbed by Homeland Security for a group they believed stretched between several countries and had smuggled over two hundred thousand firearms into the US to date.

The chief tapped the file. "It's yours."

Were her eyes bulging? Yes, they were. She gave a nod to collect herself and drew the file across the desk. It was thick, and no wonder. They'd been after these guys for months.

"I'm honored to be given the opportunity, chief. Thank you. I will do the ATF proud."

"No doubt about that in my mind, Alexander. Now off with you. You're going to be spending the next two days reading everything in that file."

"Yes. Thanks again." She got to her feet, shook his hand and with the thick folder tucked to her chest, she went to her cubicle to gather her things for home.

She was just checking on the whereabouts of her keys, when she sensed someone looming nearby.

Glancing up, she saw Mark and offered him a smile. "Congratulations again."

"I thought you'd be more bitter, Alexander. I know you wanted the promotion."

Salt. In. Wound.

She shoved it all aside and smiled wider. "The early bird gets the worm. But the second mouse gets the cheese," she quoted.

His brows puckered. "Is that your way of telling me I'm in a precarious position?"

"It's a known fact in business that when things go wrong, the people who sit in offices are blamed first. But of course, you have the best people under you, Mark. I'm happy for you and wish you nothing but the best."

Scooping up the file again, she said over her shoulder, "See you tomorrow."

Her drive home—hemmed in by traffic on the beltway heading out of DC, she shot glances at the folder on her passenger's seat. The task was big, the case one of utmost importance. Operation X was thought to be responsible for twenty-thousand guns on the streets of Chicago. Homeland was pretty damn tense about it all, with good reason. They had to put this case to bed, and she would be the one to do it.

Half an hour later, inside her apartment, she kicked off her boots and cracked open the white wine. Hell, why not? It was a celebration of sorts. She was being taken seriously, given this important case.

Not bothering with a glass, she took the bottle by the neck and the file to the living room to read.

She didn't get two pages in when she set down the bottle with a thump on her coffee table. "Son of a bitch!"

They were pairing her with some special forces from the South, a division of Operation Freedom Flag. Just what she needed — some team of gun-toting, chest-thumping guys stepping on her toes. The Ranger Ops team? Who the hell were they?

She brought up a search on her computer, but of course, it revealed nothing. Homeland would have them all flying beneath detection, and now she couldn't even test how cold the waters were before being thrown into it.

Given her choice, she would not have selected a special forces unit to assist her on this case. She would have taken trustworthy, tried and true agents and created a small group to investigate the operation.

So she was given only half control, an annoyance that she must overcome and with a smile on her damn face too. One bit of feedback Holden had given her had been that she could use her people skills to get further in her career.

She could only guess Mark Mitchum's way of charming people into getting what he wanted out of them had given him a leg-up. Well, next time, she'd be ready. Dealing with a team of cocky military men — maybe there was a woman among them too? — would be the first challenge Nealy tackled.

She got halfway through the file before her eyes grew too grainy to continue. She was just taking out her contacts for bed, when her cell rang.

"Alexander," she answered automatically.

"New information just came in."

"Mark. I see you're diving right into the new position." She pressed her brown hair back off her face.

"No time to waste. Operation X is bigger than we thought. They've captured and held one of our men hostage, and his team just recovered him."

She leaned against the sink, mind whirling.

"He was just transported to DC for medical care, and I expect you in there questioning him as soon as he's able to speak."

"Yes, right away. I'll check on him first thing in the morning and see what I can discover."

He named the hospital in Bethesda, twenty miles or so away, and she committed it to memory, taking note that the place specialized in burn treatments of armed forces after explosions.

She gripped the phone tighter, thinking of what this man might have endured at the hands of Operation X. And to think, the American government only believed they were dealing with arms trafficking, never guessing at what they were truly capable of.

"I'll see what I can find out, Mark."

"Do that. His name's Lincoln Reed."

* * * * *

The light rap on Linc's hospital room door had him cracking an eye open and lifting his head off the stiff pillow.

"Jesus," he muttered under his breath. It was her again—the ATF agent who was up his ass with so many questions about the group who'd captured him. Linc would be happy to be out of this hospital, this city and far away from her.

She'd been irritating him almost daily for weeks and always showed up when he was about to drift off to sleep.

She didn't seem to be taking the hint that he wasn't going to remember more than what he'd already shared with her either. Though she was

23

pretty in an intriguing sort of nerd-grew-up way, she knew how to get on a man's last damn nerve.

"Oh good, you're awake." Nealy Alexander sailed into the room with that self-assured walk that bugged the hell out of him.

"Not like you'd go away if I wasn't," he responded, pushing up into more of a sitting position. He was exhausted from a restless night's sleep. Either the pain from his burns had him waking with his every miniscule movement, or a nurse came in to take his vitals and check his dressings.

Alexander took up the only seat in his room, and Linc gave her the eye.

"Which is it today?" he asked. "Do you want to know more about the crate I was in or the back of the truck I was locked in?"

She gave him a flat look—the woman didn't have a bone of personality in her entire body. She leaned back in the plastic chair and crossed her legs. She always wore black trousers cut like a man's. Her button-down tops varied in color from white to pale gray, though. She really liked to party it up, this one.

He sighed and settled in for the long haul. Once she got into this position with legs crossed, she was single-minded and wouldn't leave until she had enough of his vague answers. One of these days, he was going to get up and toss her out.

A grim smile spread over his face at the thought.

She did a double-take. "What are you smiling for?"

"No reason." He waved a hand to egg her on. "Let's hear the questions so we can get this over with."

She arched a brown eyebrow, and the look in her eyes told him she didn't much care for him either. "Let's go back to the moment you were taken."

He stifled a groan. They'd been over this so many times, and he wasn't going to change his story now. What was the fucking point?

All he wanted to do was sleep for another hour before the nurse came in to bug him.

Resting his head back on the pillow, he closed his eyes.

Ahhh, silence. Pure bliss.

"Lincoln?"

He opened his eyes. "For fuck's sake, woman. Not only do you always come in when I want to sleep, but you also insist on using my full name."

"Linc. Fine," she bit off.

"I can't tell you anything more than I already have the last six times you were here." He returned her flat look, but he added a measure of lowered brows.

She one-upped him by narrowing her eyes.

"You're not leaving until I recap it, are you? Okay, here goes. Grab some water if you're thirsty, because it's gonna take a bit."

"Thanks, but I don't need anything. I just had a big lunch. I'm more than ready." She uncrossed her legs and crossed them the other direction. The buttons of her top pulled over her breasts momentarily and then released as she relaxed.

He opened his mouth and recounted the events — his team advancing on the enemy through a forest at night, knowing that they had the place rigged with land mines and other explosives to keep the OFFSUS teams at bay and from discovering that the smugglers had a shit ton of weapons ready to roll into the US through various means.

"What means?" she asked.

He rolled his eyes. "Why don't you take notes so I don't have to spell it out for you again and again?"

"I have it all committed to memory already. I'm asking because it's a known fact that the more you think of an event, the more you remember. Your mind can skip over the big details and focus on some smaller ones you might have missed the first time you told it."

"Yeah, well, there aren't any other details. You forget I've been in law enforcement my entire career before this, and I damn well remember *all* the details."

"Fine. Go on."

"Got into a skirmish, arm around my neck, being dragged backward, yada yada."

She gave a light shake of her head as if she was disappointed in him. He didn't know why, but that infuriated him.

He let out a not-so-subtle growl of annoyance. "Know what? I'm tired and you're cutting into my healing time."

At that moment, a nurse entered. She was one of his favorites because she was gentle with the treatment of the burns on his legs, unlike Nurse Killjoy, as he'd dubbed one with a heavy hand.

He gave her a smile. "Good morning, Lynn."

"Hi, Linc. Nice to see a smile on your face this morning."

From the seat against the wall, Agent Alexander gave a sniff and a huff before standing. "I'll leave you for the day, but I'll return."

"Don't make it too soon," he said in an overly cheerful tone, happy when she walked out, looking like she had a tree trunk up her ass.

He collapsed against the pillow again. "I'll just close my eyes while you change the bandages, okay, Lynn?"

"Yes, Linc. I'll try to be gentle."

"I know you will."

* * * * *

27

She was back and wearing her usual uniform dress of black pants and a white button-down shirt. Today she had the sleeves rolled up her forearms, revealing slender wrists and skin with a spattering of freckles.

He had a thing for freckles. Call it twisted but he loved a pale woman.

Linc diverted his gaze and focused on the window over Agent Alexander's head. The sky was always gray through the tinted glass hospital windows.

"Let's talk about when you were held in the crate."

Let's fucking not.

"It was wooden."

"Metal."

What the hell? Was she trying to trip him up? He'd told her it was metal.

"And you weren't able to break through it to escape."

"I've told you all this before." He threw back the sheet covering him and swung his legs over the bed, tired of lying after a month in the damn hospital. He was ready to spring this joint and be cleared to rejoin the Ranger Ops.

Agent Alexander's gaze dropped from the T-shirt he wore to the bandages covering both legs. Some of the burns were exposed to the air, the blistering done and only a twisted mass of scars left behind.

Her expression was unchanged as she stared at his burns, as if the sight of it didn't affect her at all. He didn't know how to feel about that. First off, he wanted to shock her into running out that damn door with all haste. But he also wanted to test a woman's reaction to his new look, ugly scars and all.

She raised her gaze and settled it firmly on his. He waited.

"Could you hear anyone speaking while you were locked in the crate?"

"Jesus, you're relentless. I've told you every sound was muffled. Ever been locked in a closet as a kid? No? I'm sure your parents wanted to."

She did the legs uncrossing and crossing thing, her expression bland. "I realize you're used to speaking to people any way you want, Lincoln. But—"

"Linc," he grated out.

"I'm just trying to do my job, *Linc*. Investigating Operation X is my number one priority."

"Surely, *Nealy*," he spat, "you have other people with better intel than I have. You've exhausted me enough with your eternal questioning and going in circles. I don't operate that way. I say what's on my mind *one time* and then I let it go. End of fucking story."

"I didn't realize talking was so exhausting to a former Texas Ranger who's been newly assigned to a unit of OFFSUS." She offered him a cool smile. Her pale pink lips turned upward with no guile or semblance of sincerity at all—because she was a heartless woman who didn't have her shit together on this case.

"Look." He stood, feeling more powerful than he had the last time he'd gotten to his feet. Maybe his wrath was bolstering him. Whatever—he'd take it. "I don't care if you like me or don't. I don't care if you believe me or don't. You're nothing to me, and I'm finished with this questioning. Not just for today—forever."

She stood, and they faced each other, closer than they'd ever been before, with only a foot of space between his bare feet and her plain black, rubber-soled shoes. He dragged in a deep breath.

"You've been very uncooperative during this entire month, Reed."

"And you've been annoying this entire month, Alexander."

They glared at each other. Her dark brown eyes gave him the first change of expression he'd seen from her yet, when they glimmered with animosity. Finally, he was getting a real rise from the woman, and damn, it felt good.

"Perhaps I'll have a chat with Colonel Downs about our visits."

"Go for it." If his superior officer knew this woman, he'd completely understand Linc's inability to remain civil.

She dropped a hand to her side, and he was pleased to see she curled her fingers into a fist.

He cocked his head at her, examining her features up close. Nothing remarkable — almond-shaped eyes so dark he couldn't see the centers and in contrast, paler brown hair that didn't appear to be a dye job. Her nose and mouth didn't stand out to him as anything but average.

Though her lashes were very long and curling, and she wore no makeup at all.

In fact, up close he was able to see a spattering of more freckles across her cheekbones and the bridge of her nose.

"I won't be returning, Reed."

"Good."

She slapped the mask of indifference over her face again, and the flat look she was so damn good at returned. "I wish you a speedy recovery."

"Thank you."

She skirted around him, sleeve brushing his arm on the way past. He turned to watch her walk out the door in that long-legged stride that annoyed the fuck out of him.

He wasn't sure what it was about that walk, but she left him grinding his teeth every damn time.

"Hell." He sank to the edge of the bed and ran a hand over his face and then through his short hair. He missed his cowboy hat. "I gotta get out of here before she changes her mind and comes back."

Chapter Three

Nealy threw herself back in her chair and stared at the ceiling. The little patterns of dots of the ceiling tiles gave her no help at all in this situation. There had to be another path.

But she couldn't see what.

She did not need the help of the Ranger Ops team to bring down Operation X.

She considered the hundreds of cases she'd worked on over the course of her career. With so much experience, she had this. She'd handled similar cases before.

Only, they weren't this large scale.

So it would be like working on several cases at the same time. Easy.

She looked for her car keys, but they weren't on the corner of her desk where she'd left them. She moved some files and then looked in the top drawer of her desk. Finally, she pushed backward and scanned the floor.

Sure enough, the keys were under the desk. She folded in half to reach for them, when a deep male voice sounded.

"Alexander."

She smacked her head on the underside of her desk. "Oh Jesus." *Smooth, Nealy. So smooth.* She hadn't felt like an awkward teen in at least twenty minutes.

Clapping a hand over the pain on her skull, she peered up at Mark. He was grinning, clearly having seen her embarrassing moment.

"How's the case coming?"

"Closing in." With keys in hand, she sat back and tried to look as if she dropped her keys and bashed her head off her own desk every day, meanwhile taking down huge arms traffickers.

"So, progress."

She nodded.

"And you have Ranger Ops on board."

Not exactly.

She nodded. "They've been very helpful in providing key information to get us closer to our target."

Shit—she was going to have to return to the hospital, wasn't she? Her link to the special ops team was Lincoln. Linc. What the hell ever.

"In fact, I was just heading over to the hospital now to speak with our team member."

Mark nodded. "Good work, Alexander. Keep on it."

It burned her to get a pat on the back from the man who'd scored the promotion she'd wanted, but more so when she was lying through her teeth about the helpfulness of her Ranger Ops contact.

All the way over to the hospital, she replayed her last encounter with Linc in her mind. Whether crippled by pain and the tortures he'd endured, or stronger and on the mend, he was still an asshole. Cocky, self-inflated and unhelpful to the highest degree.

Still, she had to try. Only the Ranger Ops could get her where she needed to be.

As soon as she walked into his room, he looked up. "Back again, I see. Knew you couldn't stand to stay away from me," he drawled out in that deep Texas baritone.

Dammit, she'd love to just turn around and walk back out right now, but she needed this one piece of information, and she hadn't asked it yet—hadn't thought to before.

Bracing her legs wide, she stared right back. He was good-looking, she supposed, in a rough and wild way. Muscled and handsome enough to know it. God, she hated him.

"Ask your question, Agent Alexander." He flipped the page of the magazine he was looking at.

"I'm gathering to strike."

He gave her a blank *duh* look.

"And I wondered at your best guess at their whereabouts right now. Any memory of conversations you might have overheard—"

"I told you, I couldn't hear anything in that crate." His jaw clenched hard, as it always did when he spoke about the place he'd broken out of by blowing the sides off the crate—and himself up in the process.

"When you were in the truck, then. Something might have been said—"

"There wasn't." He slapped the magazine onto the bed and swung his legs over. More of the burns were uncovered than last time, and only the worst of them still bandaged.

No Marine, soldier or integral part of a special forces unit wanted to be pitied. She concealed her reaction to the burns while he stared at her.

Seeing that look in his eyes, she raised her chin a notch. "Look, I'm trying to do my job. But forget it. You don't know anything, never did. Fine. I can handle this without you."

That brought him to his feet. Arrogant bastard.

He was tall and broad and basically a stunning specimen of manhood too. Not that she cared.

He took a step toward her, and just like last time, she held her position. No man could intimidate her— didn't he realize what ATF agents really did on a daily? She'd taken down massive bodyguards of drug dealers who ran empires. Her training required it.

"You can handle it," he repeated quietly.

"That's right." She gave a single nod.

"I beg your pardon, miss," he flicked his gaze over her, "but do you have the firepower? A sharpshooter? More weapons, ammo and explosives than them? If not, it's a losing battle, and I'll see you at your funeral."

She'd said it before, and she'd say it again—God, she hated him.

But that emotion only fueled her desire to see Operation X taken down—without the help of Ranger Ops and especially without the assistance of this irritating and cocky man.

*****

Linc hadn't put on pants in more than a month. His last pair had been melted onto him. But if slipping into cargo pants again meant he was walking out of this place, then he was eager.

He drew them up to his waist, holding his breath as he did, and was surprised to find no pain radiated through him. Relief struck, and he grinned, tugging his pants into place and buttoning the waist.

A new phone, given to him by Colonel Downs, who'd come by himself to congratulate Linc on his recovery, buzzed. He brought it to his ear, and several shouts projected into his ear.

Laughing, he held it away from his head and waited for the guys to stop.

"Welcome back, Linc!"

"Hurry home, Linc! We put your name on the scorecard and your bowling ball's waiting for you!"

He chuckled, thinking of their hangout, the Pins 'n Sins. None of them really loved bowling, but it was a good place to decompress and blow off steam. Man, he couldn't wait to get back.

"When do you fly out?"

"Sixteen hundred," he said.

"You can fit in a game tonight," said Cav.

"We'll keep your beer cold!" Jess added.

"Hurry your ass back, bro," Lennon said, leaving Linc choked up by the tone of his twin's voice.

"I'll pick you up at the airport," Shaw offered.

"That'd be good, thanks."

"No prob."

"Glad to have you back soon," Nash, otherwise known as Sully, said. "We were gettin' pretty damn sick of your replacement."

Linc was happy to hear his brothers hadn't bonded with the guy from Team Rougarou from Louisiana and edged Linc out.

After Linc ended the call, he looked around the room he'd called home for almost five weeks. No love was lost on these bland white walls, and even glancing at the chair had him thinking of his biggest annoyance in being here, more so than the constant therapy and painful debriding of his burns to promote healing.

Yup, he was ready to walk out.

He pocketed the phone and grabbed the paperwork he'd been left with. As he passed the nurse's station, several threw him waves and good wishes. Lynn came around the desk to hug him. He gave her a smile, and she said, "If you're ever in DC, stop in and say hello."

"I will."

He moved on to the elevator. As soon as he pressed the button to go down, the doors opened, and he bit off a groan.

The ATF agent stood there, prepared to step off the elevator. Seeing him, she moved back.

"Going down?"

"You just couldn't stay away, could you?" he drawled, crowding her back on purpose, though she was the only person in the elevator.

Something about her looked different today. As he pressed the button for the ground floor, he looked at her from the corner of his eye.

"You've got your walking papers," she said.

He nodded. Yeah, she was different—dare he say prettier? He couldn't put his finger on it.

He shot her a sideways glance. Same black pants, same white shirt. Same—

That was it—her hair wasn't pulled back in the slick ponytail she always wore, but instead, the strands were loose, extending down toward her breasts in thick waves.

"I'm glad you're mended. Headed back to your unit?"

"Yes," he said. "Why were you coming to see me?"

"Who said I was coming to see you?"

"You got another poor guy in the hospital you want to interrogate daily about his connection to a cell of arms traffickers?"

"No," she said dryly. "Drug smugglers." She pivoted to him, and he swore he caught a smile, but just then the elevator jolted.

She reached out to stabilize herself, and he caught her by the arm just as the entire unit came to a dead stop—and then freefell for at least six feet.

Nealy's legs went out from under her, and she sank to the floor.

The movement didn't bother Linc at all—but the close proximity of the walls did.

His breathing quickened, and he realized he was starting to sweat. It wasn't from the air being cut in here either.

Fuck, not again. He wasn't likely to find any baked goods to create a bomb a second time.

Cautiously, he reached for the elevator buttons, waiting for the unit to plummet further.

"Don't press any buttons," Nealy said.

"Why not?"

"Haven't you watched any movies? They always press all the buttons and the elevator's jammed for hours, locking them in."

Fuck. Hours. A bead of sweat ran down his nape.

He couldn't give in to his past experiences. He'd get them out of this.

He pressed the emergency call button. A second later, a woman's voice filled the elevator. "We're aware your unit has stopped, and repairmen are working on it right now. Please take a seat on the floor and try to remain calm."

She clicked off. Nealy sent him a look. "Remain calm? She's sitting at a desk and we're locked in an elevator. Simple for her to say."

"Take it easy. This sort of things happens more than you might think. They'll free us soon."

The pulse in her throat flickered rapidly. She was freckled there as well.

Shit.

And she was afraid.

The usual hard look in her eyes fled, replaced by one of worry. She bit down on her lower lip, plumping it.

It'd been a long time since he had a woman underneath him—or on top of him. When she pulled her teeth away from her lip, blood flooded into the spot, darkening it to a deeper shade of rose.

She brought her knees to her chest and cradled her head in her hands. "I don't think I like tight spaces."

"*You* don't like tight spaces?" He sank down beside her. Okay, he was starting to feel the walls close in on him too.

They stared at each other and then looked away. A strange camaraderie with her came over him. He didn't want her to see him sweat, and she was tough enough to keep him from knowing she didn't like being in this jam either.

"What are we going to do?" Her voice was too thin and high for his liking.

"I guess we wait." His own was raspier than he wanted.

She sliced a look his way. Up close, he could see golden flecks in her dark eyes.

"If I admit I'm a bit nervous, you're going to laugh and throw it in my face, aren't you?" she asked.

"Not unless you throw it in mine."

His voice took on a grittier edge. Fuck, he wasn't going to do this, was he?

Yeah, he was.

He reached for her, yanked her across his lap, and crushed his mouth over hers.

Her gasp was muffled by his kiss, but she parted her lips enough for his entrance. He took the chance to slip his tongue inside her warm, wet mouth, tasting lemon and mint as he growled out at the pure pleasure of having his hands on a woman again.

Suddenly, she yanked free, staring at him — at least until the lights abruptly cut off, plunging them into darkness.

"Fuck," she said softly.

"Yeah," he grated out. "Let's fuck."

They threw themselves at each other. Fumbling over buttons and zippers, kicking everything into a pile. He grabbed her by the waist and moved her to straddle him.

Falling still, she said, "I don't suppose you're carrying a condom."

"Babe, I'm lucky to have my legs. If you want to do this, I can guarantee I'm clean."

"I'm on birth control." Surprising him, she wrapped her arms around his neck and slanted her mouth over his. It was all the answer he needed. He slid his hands down her hips to cup her firm ass, then lifted her onto his cock.

She pushed down immediately, taking him into her clenching heat right to the hilt. He growled out his pleasure, and she echoed with a low cry that ignited him.

She began to ride him with frantic little jerks of her hips, and it wasn't enough for him. He scooped her up under the thighs and lifted her as he stood. Pressing her against the dark wall, he couldn't make out a single curve of her body in the darkness, though her lips felt plumper, she felt softer and less angled like her sharp tongue.

"Linc!" she cried as he locked her to the wall and began to fuck her fast and hard.

His balls drew up tight, so full after weeks of battling his own injuries and demons. "You're so fucking wet," he ground out, control fluttering away like smoke in a breeze. Hell, for all he know, they were surrounded by smoke and the elevator on fire. He didn't care about anything but taking his ease and giving Nealy the biggest, most memorable orgasm of her life.

Sucking her full lower lip into his mouth, he nibbled on it even as he skated a hand over her torso. Her breasts were on the smaller side but a good handful, and he wondered if she bore freckles over the tops of those as well as her nose.

He moaned. She dug her nails into his shoulders and levered herself upward on his shaft. As her body tightened around him, he closed his fingers over her nipple. The bud pebbled at his touch, and he pinched it with insistence as he sank into her again and again.

The elevator gave a jerk and fell another foot. She clutched at Linc, and he held her fast to him, breathing hard.

"If we're dying, I'm not letting you go out with anything but a smile on your face." He spun from the wall and they tumbled to the cold floor. Instantly, she wrapped her thighs around his waist and he regained his rhythm. Her lips were driving him crazy, and in

43

the dark he could almost forget she'd driven him crazy for weeks with her nonstop questions.

Damn, he was close. He had to bring her off before him.

Reaching between their bodies, he thumbed her clit. The slick nubbin was hard, the size of a pearl. If he had more time before they plummeted to their deaths, he'd go down on her.

"Oh God..." Her quiver of pleasure boosted his ego, and he applied more pressure to her clit. Then he began the slow grind — the pad of his thumb working in a tiny circle, his cock sinking in and out in a rhythm he knew would drive her to the peak fast.

He wasn't wrong. Juices flooded him. The scent of her arousal hung sweet in the air, her breasts crushed to his chest and her mouth on his. She sucked on his tongue, and he almost came right there.

Clenching his jaw, he took her the way she needed it — the way they both needed.

Her first pulsation around his cock hit out of nowhere. She was shaking apart in his arms, head thrown back on a wild cry as she contracted on his length.

He let go. The first jet of cum leaving him stole his mind, the second his sanity. He actually might have cried out her name.

Long seconds of bliss passed over him, draining his strength.

She pushed against his chest, and he realized he was crushing her with his weight.

He rolled off, remorse already seeping in. Though he couldn't see what she was doing, he heard a rustle of cloth. A garment hit him square in the face.

The lights flickered. In the single flash before darkness settled over the unit again, he caught sight of pale legs. By touch, he figured out that he was holding his shirt and managed to yank it over his head, though it might be inside out and backward, for all he knew.

A thud hit the floor next to his leg as she tossed a boot his way.

The voice came on again. "We've almost remedied the problem, and the elevator will move to the nearest floor soon."

"Shit." Nealy made a stomping noise as if she was shoving her foot into her shoe.

Linc located his jeans with his boxers still stuffed in the leg holes. He pulled on the entire mass and zipped up. His sock was inside out, but he couldn't care less and he managed to finish dressing. When the lights came on, he was bent in half tying his boot lace.

A glance over at Nealy revealed she was standing with her back against a wall and hands pressed to it, fingers splayed, and her head drooped.

She was fully dressed, and the only indication that anything had taken place between them was the way her hair swirled around her shoulders in disheveled waves and a flush over her cheeks.

The elevator began to move in the smooth, rightful way of a well-operating machine. It only lowered a few feet before the doors opened. Without a glance at Linc, Nealy stepped off.

She didn't look back and simply walked away.

* * * * *

Nealy had five tabs open on her computer tablet as she searched for near death experiences, loss of judgment during stressful situations and the statistics surrounding elevator sex.

Dear God, how had she let things go that far with Linc? She didn't even like the man. He was rude, arrogant, annoying...

And he had a very large cock she still felt the effects of. Even after a shower, she could practically feel him inside her, stretching her.

If it happened in the dark, did it stay in the dark, like the saying about Vegas?

She closed her eyes momentarily and then opened them and tossed her tablet onto the sofa next to her. Everything about the past few hours was outside her comfort zone, against her doctrine. She did not sleep with random guys, not even in college when anonymous sex was the rule.

At the memory of Linc's touch, her nipples betrayed her by bunching into two tight beads. She slapped her hands over them and groaned. This wasn't okay—she had to shake him off and move on with her day.

He was in the air by now, on route to Texas, and she probably wasn't a glimmer of a thought in his mind. He probably did this all the time.

Disgusted with herself, she got up and went to the kitchen. She wasn't remotely hungry, but the only way to get the taste of Linc's kiss out of her mouth was to eat something. She'd tried brushing her teeth, to no avail, but food would surely wipe it out.

She yanked open the freezer door and grabbed a small tray that was microwave teriyaki. It'd give her just the bad aftertaste she needed. She slit the top of the tray and shoved it into the microwave.

She leaned against the counter, tapping her foot and trying not to think of how she'd thrown herself at him.

Like some sort of desperate woman.

I am not desperate.

He couldn't hear her thoughts and wouldn't believe her anyway. To him, she was one more notch on his bedpost, a conquest. *Hey, guys, I had sex with an ATF agent in an elevator leaving the hospital. Funny, huh?* She could hear his words now.

Clenching her hands into fists, she fought back the feel of his hard muscles under her fingers and the warm steel of his cock gliding in and out of her. She'd been wet, he was right—wetter than she'd ever been with any guy or battery-operated boyfriend.

It had to be the situation. They'd allowed their fears to manifest in bodily comfort and pleasure.

God, the pleasure...

Her pussy tingled again, and the microwave beep made her spin. She yanked open the door and removed the hot tray. The smell wasn't great, a little like bad cafeteria food. She ate far too many of these after working late nights and weekends, and she didn't enjoy going out to restaurants alone. She had her share of takeout as well, but fact was, she could use a fresh meal and didn't care enough to bother preparing one for herself.

Besides, she had little in the way of fresh food and lived out of her freezer.

Okay, thinking about food wasn't stopping the waves of memory crashing over her body, pounding at her core.

Her orgasm, the way he'd ground his thumb into her clit... She folded her arms over her chest and stifled a shiver of want.

Pathetic. She had to stop thinking of Linc and the way his callused hands had moved over her with a knowledge of her body that was beyond anything she had ever experienced before. And just how did he still have rough hands after lying in a hospital for over a month, doing nothing but pressing buttons on a TV remote and flipping pages of a magazine?

She wished there had been even a spark of light in that elevator to have seen him by. The way he filled out his clothes spoke of muscle and bulk, and she had learned a lot by her sense of touch, but it left much to the imagination.

She knew what the burns on his legs looked like.

She bit down on her lip and grabbed a fork. She stood at the counter, hovering over her teriyaki chicken meal and picking through the vegetables, separating them into groupings of carrots, peppers and broccoli. She devoured each food the same way. After the carrots were gone, she moved to the peppers, tasting nothing, not really.

The worst about the entire situation was that she had cried out his name.

He called mine too.

A smug smile quirked up the corner of her lips. She chewed a bite and replayed the gritty tone of his voice as he gave up to his lust. And her name had been on his lips.

Her smile widened. At least she wasn't alone in this mistake—it had taken two, and hopefully he was sitting in a cramped airplane seat reliving their encounter and finding things to thrash himself for.

It was only fair.

In the other room, her phone buzzed. Her heart gave a hard flip-flop, and she dropped her fork with a clatter to run for her phone.

It could be Linc.

She didn't want it to be Linc.

Please don't let it be Linc.

It wasn't. "Hi, Mark. What's up?"

"Hey, I just heard about your elevator ordeal. You all right?"

Her mouth dried out. "Yes. Totally fine."

"Scary stuff. You hear of things like that happening, but you never think it will happen to you."

She never thought she'd be having elevator sex with a smoldering-hot special ops guy who she despised either.

"Yes," she said vaguely to her boss. "I'm fine and I'll be working on analyzing some of this data tonight."

"You should knock off for once, Alexander—you overwork yourself."

"Not hardly." She gave a short laugh, mostly annoyed. She wasn't some pampered princess who required a lie-down after a jarring moment, and she wasn't about to let her boss think of her that way.

"Thanks for checking in on me, Mark. I'm fine." She ended the call and collapsed onto the couch, her frozen meal forgotten.

For a moment, she found herself staring into space, her mind pitch black, as black as the inside of that elevator. She'd never had sex where she couldn't see her partner, and it had been kind of exciting, if she was honest.

The danger of a plummeting elevator coupled with an unknown partner had amplified everything. Linc probably wasn't that good in bed — her mind had made it into something it wasn't.

She sniffed and reached for her tablet again, clicking out of the windows and pulling up a database Homeland had given her access to.

Throwing herself into the work she loved, she didn't realize hours had passed until the neighbor in the next apartment came home from his late shift at work and slammed the door.

Nealy blinked away the graininess in her eyes and closed out of the database.

She didn't want to think on it much, but it was inevitable.

There was no hope for it. Her research pointed to one path.

She had to go to Texas and talk to Ranger Ops.

Chapter Four

"Damn, this is what they send me on my first fucking day back?" Linc gripped his night vision goggles and did a sweep of the area. They had a hostage situation on their hands, and yet another relative of a certain Texas politician was fighting for his life.

"You'd think this guy would throw in the towel and give up his position just to ensure his family's safety," Lennon said from beside him as he checked and double-checked his weapon.

"You can't back down against people like this." Linc threw his brother a look. "Thanks for not leaving me out there, man. I haven't said it yet."

His twin gave him an are-you-fucking-shitting-me look. "Thought about it," he bluffed. "You're a pain in the ass. And I don't think you ever returned my favorite vinyl to me."

The vinyl LP of Lennon's favorite 80s hair band was still on the turntable in Linc's house. He had no intention of returning it to his brother, but now he was feeling some brotherly love, he might consider it.

"On your eleven, Linc. You good to go?" Sully's voice projected into his ear through the comms unit. The last time he'd heard from his captain in this way, he'd been jerked off his feet and woken in the back of a truck smelling pig shit.

"Ready to roll." He slanted a look at Lennon, who gave a nod.

They ran forward in a burst of speed. In seconds, they had one of the guards on the ground. Then they hit the door. Linc stood back while Lennon shot the lock off using a silencer on his weapon.

The door gave way, and Linc slipped inside, swinging his head right and left, weapon at the ready and his finger hovering over the trigger. He was relieved to know he wasn't having any traumas from his last experience. Shaw had suffered for months after killing a youth who'd been about to shoot him, and Linc had been somewhat afraid of that after his ordeal.

Of course, he wasn't likely to be locked in a crate again. Though, he had known a moment of panic in the elevator—right before he and Nealy had gotten naked.

"On your three," Lennon breathed into the comms.

Linc pulled up and took the shot. The guy hit the concrete floor, slumping over so it looked as if he might have fallen asleep on the job.

With Lennon at his back, they breached another section of the building. Voices projected from behind a metal door. Suddenly, Linc thought of the crate and how everything had sounded like he was hearing it from under water. That brought him to thinking about Nealy's relentless questioning.

And how hard and wet her clit had been beneath his thumb.

Focus, he told himself.

"Incoming."

He spun in time to see two men bearing down on them, weapons drawn.

He and Lennon were faster.

Lennon stepped over one Linc had taken out. "Thanks, bro."

"Don't mention it."

They drew up to the door. Linc pulled out a camera to look through the crack. There, roped to a chair, was the politician's loved one. A cousin or some shit, but one he was close to allegedly. The man's lips were moving, but Linc couldn't make out a thing he said.

"Mic it," Lennon whispered.

Linc fiddled with a setting and had the sound in all the Ranger Ops' ears. As the cousin blubbered about how his family had money and could drop it anyplace the kidnappers wanted, Linc silenced it once more. It was time to go in.

Half an hour later, they walked out with the cousin in tow, put him into the front of an armored car and sent him on his way. Then they had to make a call to collect the bodies.

Lennon clapped him on the back, and Linc pivoted his head to look at him. "You did good for your first day back. Any pain?"

Linc shook his head. They stopped walking as an SUV pulled up. A window rolled down, and Linc stepped forward, thinking to see the politician.

He drew up short as his gaze fell on the woman behind the lowered glass. Their stares connected, and lurid images flashed through his mind as a dark heat crawled through his groin.

He pushed out a sigh. "Now you're showing up on my jobs?"

She narrowed her eyes. "I need to speak to your captain."

Like hell, was Linc's first thought. Suddenly, he realized Sully would be left with the headache and Linc wouldn't have to deal with the annoying woman.

She turned in profile and said something to the driver. Then she got out. Beside him, he felt Lennon go still as he stared at the woman.

Oh hell no. His brother could not be looking at the ATF agent as a woman, could he? She was plain at best.

Except Linc remembered very well how soft her curves had felt under his hands in the dark elevator.

And how pretty he'd thought she was before stepping onto the elevator.

She looked to his brother, and Lennon extended a hand. "You must be Lennon," she said.

He grinned and clasped her hand.

"Yeah, my twin and the guy who doesn't have time to stand around talking to you," Linc cut in, shouldering his brother aside.

Lennon and Nealy stared at him. At that moment, the rest of the guys approached, bulked out with gear and grins on their faces as they ripped on each other.

Linc pointed out Sully. "That's the guy you wanna talk to."

He turned and walked away. A second later, Lennon jogged up beside him.

"So… she have freckles?"

"Shut up, Lennon."

"That's a yes. Freckled everywhere?"

"Dude, you're about to get decked." He continued on to the Ranger Ops SUV, peeling his sling holding his automatic over his head.

"Another yes."

"Look, she's an irritating woman who came by the hospital in DC asking me questions about the guys who took me."

"Oh shit."

"Yeah. I don't have fuzzy feelings toward her."

"Sure looked that way when you saw her."

Fuck—just what Linc did not need. He hoped to hell Nealy hadn't noted anything of the like, because it was false to the max. There weren't feelings involved—it was sex in an elevator, and since then, he'd often wondered why he'd even done it. He liked women, but he wasn't one to take advantage, especially if he disliked the woman. He had *some* moral code, after all.

They reached the SUV, and Linc opened the back to stow away his weapon. After that, he made the mistake of tossing a glance over his shoulder—to see Nealy looking at him.

* * * * *

Great—Linc had caught her staring after him, and now she looked like a groupie or a lost puppy or something equally as bad. She bit off a mental groan and returned her attention to Captain Nash Sullivan. The big man was cordial enough, though she could see he wanted to hurry and get to her reason for wanting to speak to him.

She rushed through her own introduction and then got right to the point.

She only half took note of Linc approaching again.

Okay, maybe a little more than half.

"I have been given direct orders to join forces with Ranger Ops with the directive to bring down Operation X."

"Jesus," Linc muttered. Nealy stared at him, hoping his balls shriveled up and fell off from her glare alone.

"You know about this?" Linc asked his captain.

Sullivan gave a nod. "I got the call from Downs this morning." He directed his gaze to Nealy. "I haven't heard a peep about Operation X for over a month. What makes you think they aren't long gone, retreated to Mexico?"

She appraised him. "You seem like a smart guy—do they ever just retreat?"

A ghost of a grin crossed Sullivan's face. "We'll take action when we get the call." He narrowed his eyes. "Do you know something I don't?"

She nodded. "I've got intel that there's a flash drive containing enough information to find every man and every weapon they have on its way into the United States—and where to find it. But it means breaching a rather precarious and heavily guarded position."

"At that time, you can give me the information and we'll handle it."

She shook her head before the words were completely out of his mouth. "My direct order is to get the flash drive into my hand. You get me in, and I retrieve it."

He gave a stiff nod. "Like I said, we'll take action when we get the call. I'll let you know when the time comes. But be warned—what we do ain't for the faint of heart."

She drew up. She'd been facing the thinking that a woman couldn't achieve or stomach the same things as men all her life, and so far, she'd shown she could hold her own.

Suddenly, out of the corner of her eye, she caught Linc taking a step closer. Her stomach tensed. Or maybe that was much lower. Ugh, here she was arguing that she was strong enough to hang with the guys while lusting over one.

But maybe that didn't make her weak or the wrong sex to do the job—it just made her human.

Linc focused on her. "Honey, take the night off— we are."

She gaped at the man, more audacious—and dammit, more handsome—than he had been in the hospital. Coming off his current mission, he was rugged, decked out in camo and with streaks of paint across his face to disguise himself in the night.

He also wore a thunderous look that made her want to kick him in the balls.

"Look, Linc—"

"I need to debrief and then shower. You can join me—but we won't be doin' much talking."

What. A. Fucker.

Calling her out in front of the other men she wanted to respect her? Acting as if he was God's gift to womankind?

She gave him her best glare, one that usually made grown men look away.

"Man, that was a little harsh," Sullivan was saying to Linc.

She spun back to the car that had brought her here. Fury ricocheted through her body, along with something darker, more disturbing.

That something was lust.

She was turned on, and damn if she'd let him see how hard her nipples were through her top.

She yanked open the car door and slipped in.

Sullivan put a hand on the door, preventing her from closing it. "I'm sorry for my teammate. He's an asshole sometimes."

She looked past him to Linc and said, "I need your assistance in this matter, but I refuse to work in these conditions."

If there was any way around working with Ranger Ops, she needed to find it. If she never set eyes on Lincoln Reed again, she'd hire a bunch of parade floats to make a celebration of it.

"We'll speak to you tomorrow. All of us," Sullivan added, tossing a look over his shoulder at Linc. "Come to our base." He recited an address and then closed the door for her. He tapped the side of the vehicle, and the man hired as her driver set the car in motion.

How was it possible that every time she thought of Linc, she was irritated—and at the same time

60

turned on? He'd muddled the emotions in her mind with the elevator moment, but she was just as much to blame.

Her loss of judgment was going to haunt her every single time she looked at the man, and that was inevitable if they were combining forces.

* * * * *

Linc's muscles were a little more tired than usual after a mission. Made sense, since he'd spent over a month being idle. But that wasn't why he was wide awake at two in the morning.

Nealy was here in the city, and he couldn't get her out of his head. Which was ridiculous, considering he didn't even like her. Okay, so he liked *some* parts of her. Her mouth was just fine as long as she wasn't using it to talk.

He grunted and rolled onto his side. It was heaven to be in his own bed, but sleep was far from him.

He knew exactly why she was here, and the Ranger Ops would accommodate her by joining ranks to deal with Operation X. They had the muscle and firepower while she had the backing of federal law. Together, they'd be unrivaled, and it was exactly what they needed to bring down those fuckers who'd held him in a crate.

Shifting his jaw, he scowled at the window. The blinds were drawn down, but through a crack, a streetlight glowed blue in the darkness. He couldn't see the sky, and for a born and raised country boy, that was a problem.

His mind skipped from the present to his childhood. He and Lennon raised by a momma who worked so much just to keep them fed. Their days had been peaceful, living in a rural area where they could ride bikes to the creek to fish or swim in a farmer's pond without him knowing. One time Lennon had left his socks on the bank of a pond, and the farmer had called their momma to tell her to keep her boys off his land. But she'd only told him boys would be boys and at least they were staying out of real trouble.

She always had their backs, and it had been a long time since Linc had visited her. As soon as he could break away, he'd go, spend some time just sitting in a field breathing in the scent of grasses and staring at the big Texas sky. Maybe horseback ride through a canyon.

Yeah, getting in touch with nature was just the thing he needed to calm his soul.

He flipped over onto his other side to stare into the darkness. After a bit, his eyelids grew heavier, and he was about to drop off to sleep when his phone buzzed.

Only one person would be calling at this hour — his captain.

Wide awake now, he took the call. In five minutes, he was decked out in cammies. When he got to the rallying point, six dark shapes stood by the SUV. He parked his car and got out, staring at the outlines in the darkness. He made out Lennon's form easy, and Jess had his cowboy hat on.

But the smaller figure...

With a jolt, he realized exactly who it was. He remembered the lines of that body in darkness like no other.

Fucking hell—Nealy wasn't serious about imposing herself on this trip, was she?

His second thought as he strode across the parking lot was where the hell she'd fit in the vehicle. The back was crowded with Cav and Jess, and he and Lennon took up the middle row.

That left her crunched between them—or in Linc's lap.

He growled as he drew to a stop, his glare on Nealy. She was dressed in black cargo pants and a black T-shirt, both of which showed off more of her figure than he'd ever seen. Even in the darkness, he made out the curve of her breasts he remembered so well, and his dick hardened.

Dammit.

He swung his head toward Sully. "You invite her?"

The captain gave a small shake of his head in response, probably sensing Linc was about to blow.

"Actually, you're all with me. I have direct orders to go into this place." Nealy's voice drilled into Linc's psyche.

"Jesus. Are you kidding me?"

"Not a bit."

"Does your superior want you killed? Because that's what you're facing if you're with us." He eyed her.

She didn't even pale at his words as most women would. Instead, she drew up taller. "I've got access to things you don't, and I know things about this group."

Compressing his lips, he gritted out, "Woman, anything you know can be passed on to us. Let us do our jobs. Go back to your hotel and your bed."

She set her hands on her hips and faced him. Even in the dark, he saw the anger on her face. "I am highly trained in investigating violations to federal laws relating to firearms and explosives, both of which we'll be dealing with if you ever stop dragging your feet and get into the damn SUV."

"Woman, you cross too many lines as it is. The last thing we need is—"

"Linc." Sully's heavy hand came down on his shoulder, cutting off his words. "She's got a valid tactical layout for us. Easy in, take control, easy out."

He ground his molars against anything more he wanted to say. His captain's word was the final one, and he'd just have to live with it.

"Fine." He grabbed the door and yanked it open, launching inside and fastening his seatbelt.

Sully came to the door and stared at him. "You good, man?"

Linc leveled his gaze at him. "Why wouldn't I be?"

"You just came back and haven't had rest—"

"As long as I can hold a weapon and crawl, I'm good." He reached for the door handle, and Sully stepped back so he could slam the door.

A second later, a tight little body slid onto the seat beside him. Linc glanced down at the small gap of an inch between their legs, aware of the scent of her shampoo. The best thing he'd ever smelled in this vehicle full of dirty, sweaty men who shared a love of burritos.

He let out the breath he realized he was holding and turned his head to the window, looking through tinted glass to the black of night.

When Lennon crowded in the other side, taking over much of the seat, Linc felt Nealy's thigh brush his.

She moved it, but that left her knees crunched together. She'd be cramped by the time she got out at their destination, but it served her right.

During the entire ride, he remained silent, unwilling to add to the conversation taking place about who had a better bowling handicap. Nealy was equally as quiet, her arms folded over her chest. Once in a while, he saw her fingers pluck at the fabric of her T-shirt, and he took it as a sign of her nerves. Though on the surface, she appeared as composed as any of the Ranger Ops.

Damn ballsy of her, to be coming along with them. He didn't care if it was an order that came directly from Colonel Downs. Linc knew her training gave her enough ability to handle herself in a chase, in a shootout and probably provided enough physical prowess to take down a man much larger than her. That didn't mean she was prepared for the shit they were about to do.

They were headed to Chihuahua, Mexico, and that wasn't easy terrain even without being laden down with gear.

Judging by the landscape, they were about to employ their training in cliff climbing. At the top of a cliff was a glimmer of light from the multimillion-dollar mansion that was their destination.

"Damn, these people got the money and brains to position their house in a place nobody can breech without climbing gear," Shaw said.

"That's the plan. Two at a time until we reach the top."

Linc, prepared for the physical challenge, moved to the back and began pulling gear out. The equipment took longer to rig up than reaching the top would.

He sliced a look at Nealy. "Ever done this before?"

She nodded. "For recreation, but I'm confident I'll be fine."

Looking over her head, he said to Sully, "She's with me."

She opened her mouth to retort, but Linc caught her eye, and she snapped it shut.

He was just feeling like he might have won that battle, when she said, "Once we reach the top, though, I'm going in."

"You," he said flatly, clipping the carabiners into place.

"We aren't only going in after men, Linc. Your team can take care of the threat while I search for the flash drive."

"Where exactly is this flash drive? How do you locate it in that place, when it probably has nineteen bedrooms?"

She fiddled with her own rigging, tugging to ensure it was tight. He watched her do this, making sure she was outfitted properly and wouldn't be breaking her pretty neck.

She flicked a glance at him.

"Where?" he demanded.

"My source says it's plastered into a wall."

"And you're going to find it how?"

Her focus moved from her ropes to Linc. "I was given information on what to look for."

"And when you do find it? How are you getting it out of the drywall? Are you going to shoot up the drywall so you can reach in and extract it?"

"I'll figure it out when I see it," she said.

He breathed through his nose slowly to keep from grabbing her and hogtying her in the vehicle until he got back.

He'd be nice, though, and leave a window rolled down.

* * * * *

Nealy needed all the concentration she had to get up that cliff face. The climbing part wasn't as difficult as it was to keep her eyes off the man in front of her. Linc went hand over hand like a wild beast, and it was difficult not to stare in awe at his physical prowess.

When she reached the top a short time after him, he stuck out a hand for her to take. She ignored it and heaved herself over the ledge. The place was dead quiet, and the only lights were a few low-watt security ones around the perimeter of the home.

Allegedly owned by one of the masterminds behind the weapons trade, this man was responsible for bringing hundreds of thousands of automatic weapons into the US. And she was going to be an integral part of stopping it from continuing.

She needed this on her resume.

Ahead of her, Linc flicked two fingers in a direction. She followed the gesture, watching as Ranger Ops dealt with two guards on a door. Then two of their team slipped into the home. Linc nodded and took off after them. In a crouched position with her weapon at the ready, she ran behind.

Her heart was drumming loudly in her ears, but she'd ignored her physical response to danger many, many times. In her ear, the comms unit she wore gave a staticky sound.

"Dammit, not again," one of the guys said on a whisper of a breath.

She followed the group through an inner courtyard and to another door. She spotted the guard there a split second before Linc clamped onto a pressure point on his neck and the man collapsed.

One of the Ranger Ops men bound and gagged him with the swift precision that told her they'd done this a time or ten.

"Alexander, what's the coordinates of the mark?" Linc's voice filled her ear.

He wasn't looking at her, and hearing his voice gave her an odd sense of intimacy, similar to what she'd felt in the dark elevator.

"You're not going in without me."

"Fine. Let's go—now."

She let him clear the way through the house, sneaking past a dining room with grand, contemporary furniture and polished silver, both gleaming in the low moonlight streaming through the windows. And another room, all modern angles and large art pieces.

Finally, she stopped him. "We're getting close." She glanced over the wall, searching for a small imperfection that would be hiding a cutout.

He moved with a slow, rolling stealth that reminded her that she wasn't playing in the kiddie pool anymore. Ranger Ops was the real deal, and she was proud to be among them today.

They sidestepped into the room, Linc on high alert and her using her flashlight to scope out every inch of the wall.

"You never told me how the hell you got this information, Alexander," he breathed out, barely audible.

"A team of agents dig up the intel, and my director feeds it to me." When she'd gotten the call from Mark on her journey from DC to Texas, she'd committed every word to memory, locked into her mind.

"Here," she said.

At that moment, a Ranger Ops man spoke into their comms. "Target is roaming."

Her stomach knotted, and she jerked to look at the door, expecting an enemy to walk through it.

"I think it's right here," she whispered, poking a finger at a spot on the wall.

He stared hard. "I think you're wrong."

She glared. "I was told it's a crescent-shaped divot in the wallpaper."

His brows drew together as he shook his head.

Without warning, Linc cocked a fist and punched through the plaster—a different spot of plaster. The noise seemed deafeningly loud in the silent space. Nealy stared as he yanked his hand back out and uncurled his fingers to show her he had it. "Let's go," he rasped.

He led the way as they booked it out of the house. A shot fired. Then another.

"Shit's gettin' dirty." The voice was so similar to Linc's that it must be his twin's.

Linc jerked his head for Nealy to follow. When she didn't seem to be in the position he wanted her, he grabbed her by the shoulder and shoved her down just as a hailstorm of bullets sprayed over them. He flattened his heavy body over hers, crushing the breath right out of her.

She managed to get her weapon hand free and take aim, but before she could squeeze off a shot, Linc unloaded. The explosion over her head would ensure she was wearing hearing aids by the time she hit thirty-five.

She was dragged to her feet. Everything blurred past her as they sprinted out of the house. Something stung the back of her leg, and she let out a hiss.

"Fuck, are you hit?" Linc tossed her a look and grabbed her. His hard latch on her hip and shoulder were nothing compared to her hitting the ground hard. She looked up to see a shield of foliage in front of her.

Linc hit the dirt beside her. "Cover your head. Cav's blowin' the place."

She picked her head up to ask if they were at a safe enough distance, and he shoved her down, planting a hand over her head and holding her cheek to the ground. She shook him off enough to lock her hands over her head.

When the explosion hit, she was damn glad Linc had thrown her behind the shield of tall, thick bushes.

Her ears echoed with the reverberations.

Then male laughter flooded into her comms unit.

"Anybody got a marshmallow?" one guy asked.

"No, but we can put your dick on a stick and roast it, Jess."

Deep laughter followed.

She raised her head and found Linc sitting up, grinning at her. She pushed upward, stunned that she could after the shock of the blow. Her mind didn't catch up as quick.

Before she could think of what to do next, he wrapped a hand around her nape, yanked her in and planted a kiss square on her mouth.

Chapter Five

Linc noticed Nealy wasn't trying her best to keep her thigh from touching his in the vehicle. Maybe that kiss had broken down some barricade and softened her up.

It didn't soften him, though—he had never been harder. His dick was strangled behind his fly, and he couldn't even adjust it without garnering comments from the other guys, so he rode miles in discomfort.

She shifted positions, pressing her hip to his. The pressure was driving him crazy, and he gritted his teeth.

The post-mission party atmosphere in the SUV had died down, and everyone retreated to their own thoughts. Linc found his own thoughts drifting to getting out of this vehicle, grabbing Nealy by the hand and taking her home with him. He also had visions of treating himself to a breakfast of her straddling his face.

He must have released some noise, because she sent him a glance. His gaze targeted her mouth— were her lips always that plump or had she taken a hit to make them swell that way? She hadn't indicated any injury when he'd kissed her back behind the shrub screen.

As he looked on, she ran the point of her tongue over her lower lip. His insides grabbed.

A bump in the road jostled them together, and she caught herself by bracing a hand on his thigh. Heat traveled up his leg to his groin, leaving a trace of desire so strong he had to clench his jaw.

Quickly, she snatched her hand away. But the damage was done.

When they finally rolled back into town, she jumped out the door after Lennon and made a beeline to the waiting car she must have summoned.

"Hold up, Alexander," Linc called out.

She stopped but didn't turn. He caught up and said, "You're not getting in that car. My car's over there."

Her chest rose and fell. "Linc."

"Just get in my car, Nealy." His voice took on a rough edge.

Still, she hesitated.

"Please."

She pivoted her head to meet his stare. Need did a slow, dirty crawl through his system.

"Look," he said. "You're coming home with me and I'm tearing all your clothes off. Then you're spending the night sitting on my face. We can leave the lights out so you can pretend it's not happening, if that's your preference. But we're doing this."

Without waiting for her response, he took off to his car in the dark corner of the lot. Seconds later, he saw the driver pull out and make a left turn. Nealy jogged up to the passenger's door, and Linc cut off a grin.

The drive was as silent as he expected it to be, with Nealy sitting stiff and primly with her knees together as if he was suggesting he go down on her before ever reaching home. Her hands were balled on her lap, but he did nothing to put her at ease.

Soon enough.

Twenty minutes later, he used his key code to enter the gates of the apartment complex he lived in. He rolled through the roads of the complex and hit a remote to open his garage door.

"Your brother doesn't live with you, does he?" she asked in a quiet voice.

He looked at her. "I wouldn't bring you home if he did."

After parking and securing the door shut, he led her up a short flight of stairs leading to the entry of his apartment. The place smelled a bit stale from being shut up, but nothing a few open windows wouldn't fix. He kicked off his boots and wrinkled his nose at the scent wafting up. "First, a shower's in order." He cocked a brow at her. "Join me?"

She fidgeted, as if uncertain if she should keep her own boots on in order to bolt out the door again or give in to the desire he saw burning in her eyes.

He took control, advancing on her and backing her up against the wall. Her breaths came hard and fast, and she ran her tongue over her lips again.

He let out a growl. "Let me make this easy on you, babe. I'm going to take you into my big shower and soap you all over, making sure I get... every... single... sweet spot." He pitched his voice low and let his words wash over the shell of her ear.

She shivered.

"Then I'm going to take you to my bed, stretch out, and pull your knees up around my ears right before I plunge my tongue into your soaking wet, hot, tight, needy, aching pussy."

Another shudder worked its way through her, and she braced a hand on the wall by her side to hold herself up.

He leaned away to look into her eyes. "Do you accept the challenge?"

A spark lit in her eyes, and a flame jumped in his core.

He pushed away from the wall. "Good." He walked away, and she trailed behind. He flipped on a light in the hallway and then the bathroom. There, he reached for his shirt and pulled it overhead.

She was staring at his chest, breaths still coming faster than they should be if she was unaffected.

Her gaze dropped to the front of his pants—and she saw how far from unaffected he was.

Giving her the show she never got in the dark elevator, he unbuckled his pants with slow flicks of his fingers. He slid them down his body, letting the cargo pants puddle at his ankles. He stepped out and cupped his shaft through his underwear, molding the cloth to it and showing off the length, girth and way it curved up in its hardened state.

"This was inside you, babe, and it will be again. Get out of those clothes."

She dipped her gaze to take in the healing burns on his legs.

"I'm fine. Don't worry about it."

"All right," she said on a puff of a sigh.

He watched her reach for her top. When she peeled away the fabric to reveal an expanse of creamy pale skin of abdomen, chest and breasts, it was his breaths coming faster.

With lowered lids, he watched her pull off a sports bra, letting her breasts bounce free.

He swallowed hard. Perky. A handful each. Fucking just right.

His cock swelled, surging against his underwear.

Her brown eyes burned into his as she went for her pants. A second later, she stood before him, bare. Her navel bore a tiny gold stud, which shocked him for some reason.

Below that... Jesus. He gathered a breath, but his lungs wouldn't fill with air.

Her pussy was shaven, the mound a ripe peach and the tiniest bud of her clit peeking from the top of her thickened lips.

He hit his knees in front of her. Grabbed those rounded hips and yanked her in. The second his tongue hit her juicy folds, they shared a groan and he wondered if they weren't more friends than enemies at this point.

* * * * *

Nealy threw her head back on a cry of pleasure as Linc dipped his tongue in and out of her pussy, using short flicks that were driving her wild. She'd fist his hair if he had enough of it, so she held on to his ears and guided him... up and down, back and forth.

He raised his head to grin at her with lips drenched with her juices, but she shoved him between her legs once more. He rumbled a laugh, and she found joy bubbling from her too.

He nudged her thighs apart to bury his head deeper. When he didn't seem to be happy enough with that, he grabbed her hips and lifted her onto the edge of the sink as if she weighed nothing, before lowering his mouth to her pussy again.

He licked up the seam and circled her bud. She dropped her head forward, unable to look away from the gorgeous sight of a beautiful man eating her pussy. A spasm clenched her inner muscles, and she released a flood of arousal.

"Mmm." He lapped at it with slow deliberation, holding her gaze as he did. That alone could rip the rug out from under a girl—he was fucking her with his eyes as much as his mouth.

"Lick me again," she demanded on a rasp.

He flattened his tongue and drew a line in a long slurp from bottom to top. Then pulled away to do it a second time.

Reaching between her legs, she pressed apart her outer lips to reveal the pink inner folds. "Here," she urged.

He growled and drew a zigzagging pattern over the exposed folds with his insanely hot tongue. A second spasm hit her, and she gulped on a cry.

"Give me your fingers," she begged, pulling her lips open wider to urge him inside.

"Fucking hell, babe, you're a dirty girl who knows what you want, aren't you?" He didn't wait for a reply—she didn't have one anyway, because she'd never been this way with anybody but Linc.

He smoothed two fingertips through her juices and made a show of slowly sinking them inside her.

Her body clutched at his digits, which he pressed upward against her soft inner wall. She parted her legs farther and cried out on a long moan that revealed just how much she was unraveling for this man.

Seeing him in the flesh, with the lights on, was totally doing it for her. In fact, she was right there, on the ledge of ecstasy, poised to jump.

She'd climbed a cliff with this man, seen him stride into a room and punch a hole in the wall to extract a flash drive—how the hell had he known where to find it, anyway? After that, he'd shielded her from a spray of bullets right before throwing her behind a screen to survive a blast as the multimillion-dollar house clinging to the cliff exploded.

After that, she would have done anything to be here with him right now, and she was too far gone to keep that a secret.

She pushed her hips upward to force his fingers deeper. He accommodated her, splaying his hand over her ass to give her every inch right to the knuckles. As he sucked her clit between his lips, her sensitive nerves hit a new high.

"Linc, I'm close." With a hand on the back of his head, she pushed him down to her pussy hard. "Don't stop!"

He vibrated some answer she couldn't make out, because she couldn't stop the cries bursting from her throat. When her orgasm hit, she was looking into his eyes.

And dammit, she did it again—said his name.

* * * * *

80

He wasn't making it through a shower, to the bed or even to the bathroom floor right now. Nope—he was fucking her right here on the vanity.

She reached for his underwear and shoved them down. His cock jumped free, and she curled her fingers around his length, drawing it right to her center.

"Kiss me," she demanded.

Dipping his head, he claimed her lips at the same moment he sank deep into her core.

She cried out again, but he went still, closing his eyes, every slick second he'd fucked her in that elevator rushing back at him.

He planted his hands on her knees and rocked his body into hers, balls slapping her skin. Fuck, she was tight, hot, sucking him in. And her flavors on his tongue drove him on toward a massive ending that would probably land him back in the hospital.

Setting a determined rhythm, he sank his cock into her again, drawing her tight into his arms as he did and angling his head to deepen the kiss.

The passion warring inside him was completely new. Maybe it was post-mission fucking doing it or the fact that he'd wanted more after that elevator episode, but he wasn't stopping until they both collapsed.

She wrapped her thighs around him and looped her arms over his neck. When she delivered a nipping bite to his lip, he groaned into her open mouth. He'd never had a woman come apart so completely for him as she just had when he was licking her pussy. And the demands she'd made... fuck, who knew a little wildcat lived in her boring uniform of black pants and white button-down shirt? Her dull black shoes didn't reveal the depth of this woman.

His balls tightened against his body as he thrust into her once more. That burning sensation began at the base of his spine. He had to get her off fast before he blew, and he already knew what method to use.

* * * * *

When Linc pressed the pad of his big thumb over her clit at the same moment he ground his hips, it was all over for Nealy. A wave of pleasure the size of the big Texas sky struck, knocking her flat. As every contraction stretched into a bigger one, she threw herself into the kiss.

Then his hot cum hit her inner walls, and she found herself clinging to the man as he came apart for her.

Inside her.

God, what was it about having unbridled, bare sex with Linc that just hit all her high spots? She didn't have a type—but he had to be it. She didn't have a fantasy about sex—but he delivered.

He gathered her up, kissing her with all the intensity he had before his orgasm. He turned for the shower and stepped inside the glass enclosure with her still in his arms and his cock still hard in her pussy.

Leaning his forehead into hers, he gave a low grunt. "I can't quit fucking you."

To prove his point, he rocked his hips. She wiggled in his hold, feeling insanely small surrounded by all this muscle.

"Linc, I want to taste you."

Her words fell over him, making him as still as a marble statue of David. Except he was much hotter and more built than Michelangelo's art.

She wasn't sure if he was going to let her take him in her mouth and deliver all the mind-blowing pleasure he'd given her minutes before, until he drew her up and off his cock. Her feet hit the shower floor, and she lowered herself to her knees.

With his sculpted thighs in front of her face, she was even more turned on, and she was not a woman to go ga-ga over a male physique. She worked with men, tough men, guys who hit the gym twenty hours a week just to stay on top of their game. But Linc was a totally different caliber from those men.

She stretched her hands over each thigh and leaned in, lips parted over the tip of his straining erection. The scent of man, musk and her own arousal mingled on him, a heady cocktail that had her pussy tingling for more of his touch.

Not yet—she wanted him in her mouth. All of him.

She sank over him slowly, tightening her lips to learn every ridge of his shaft. When he filled her mouth to full capacity, he let out a groan and palmed her head. She drew a breath through her nose and went all the way—sucking him into the back of her throat until her lips hit the short coarse hairs of his body.

He was fully seated in her mouth. And she was fully satisfied.

She drew on him with a small pull of her lips, and he grunted, a low noise igniting her.

Wiggling closer, she reached up to cup his heavy balls in one hand and withdrew on his arousal.

"You're killing me, babe. I'm going to drain my cock into those plump lips if you don't stop."

She hoped he did. Then if she never saw him again after today, she'd be more than satisfied that she'd done everything there was to do with Linc.

Well, there are more things, her mind spoke up. *Sex in public, sex in a bed. Sex in an elevator... oh wait, did that.*

She took him right to the base again. His abs strained, and the entire six-pack of muscles—plus a few extras the man owned—popped out in ridged finery. She opened her eyes and took in everything about him. When she'd sucked him only a few moments, he had hold of her hair, twisting it up into his fist and tugging on the strands in a way that shouldn't delight her but it was fucking sexy as hell.

He drew her head back to look into her eyes. "Look at me while you suck my cock."

Apparently, she wasn't the only person who could make demands.

She held his gaze and deliberately sucked in his impressive length once more. When she withdrew, he churned his hips, swirling the tip of his cock on her tongue. She opened her mouth wide, letting him do as he pleased with her.

The idea was shocking. She was not a woman to give up control, but with Linc, it was a mutual need for pleasure driving them, and it left behind no remorse or shame whatsoever. She could stay here on her knees, pleasuring him with her mouth, until he pulled her up and did as he wished with her.

She hoped it was bending her over and fucking her against the shower wall.

She fondled his balls, and he sank into her mouth again. Cupping her cheek on one callused palm, he held her gaze. Her insides fluttered, and she was so keyed up, so close to her own release just from serving Linc that the scantest touch of her clit would set her off.

She reached between her legs.

"Oh fuck… That's it, touch your clit for me. Rub it while you suck my cock."

Getting into it more, she pinched her clit between her fingers and made the short, jerky movements that always got her to the finish line. Linc's cock stiffened even more, shoving at the back of her throat. She swallowed her cry of bliss as the orgasm hit her.

A third in what... half an hour? It must be a world record.

Her scattered thoughts fragmented even more as the first shot of his cum hit her throat. Swallowing around him, she focused enough to give him the end result they both wanted. He rocked his hips faster and faster as he unloaded and she drew out her own orgasm with light flicks of her fingertips over her sensitive nubbin.

When he pulled her to her feet, she didn't know if she had enough muscle left to support herself. But he lashed her to him and kissed her, and she found the strength to not only stand but rub against his body.

He growled into her mouth before pulling back. "You taste like me."

"And you taste like me."

They stared into each other's eyes.

"I want more," he said.

"So do I."

She had little recollection of the shower itself— water, soap bubbles and a lot of lips and tongue in between. Somehow, she landed on cool, crisp sheets, spread eagle on his bed with Linc's tongue poised at her folds again and his eyes boring into hers.

"Say my name as I thrust my tongue into your pussy, babe. Say it for me."

"Why?" she managed as her body spiked with desire.

"Because I can't stop hearing it in my dreams since the elevator."

* * * * *

Linc was accustomed to waking alone, but he was surprised when he did. He hadn't even asked this girl to leave before dawn.

Actually, he was pissed.

Nealy had left in the middle of the night without a word. Worse, he'd slept through it. He didn't know which disturbed him more.

Maybe it was for the best that he hadn't woken next to a sexy female. He'd be distracted, wanting to run his hands all over her again.

Yeah, it was best she left without him asking her to. If they had to work together again, that could cause tension. Besides, he had errands, some laundry to do, and he'd like to go for a run later if he felt up to it.

Shrugging off the entire episode with Nealy was the thing to do. Nothing had changed, right?

He'd just had the most insanely dirty-hot night of passion of his life.

Just brushing his teeth reminded him of fucking her on the sink. Then in the shower. And her sucking him.

Ugh, he had to fucking stop. So he'd screwed a woman a few times. Nothing new.

With a canvas bag of laundry in hand, he walked down to the common area of the apartment complex to the coin laundry. There, he fed machines quarters and little boxes of powder, and he flipped through messages on his phone.

One from his momma, stating that the neighbors just had a new foal, and her gushing over how cute it was. He put away his phone. He missed his momma and the country. He'd thought about it a lot while trapped in that crate, and later in the burn unit when she couldn't come and see him.

When would he be able to break away and visit? After Ranger Ops' raid the previous night, there was sure to be another strike, and they'd be called out.

That brought his mind to Nealy again and the flash drive he'd retrieved. What had happened to it after he'd given it to Sully?

He punched a button and dialed his captain.

"Dick," Sully answered with a laugh in his tone. "You miss me or somethin'?"

"Yeah, I do," Linc responded.

"Nevaeh and I were just about to head out on horseback. You should come up sometime."

"I will."

"You keep sayin' that and never do."

"I've been missing the country life, so I'll definitely take you up on the offer soon. That isn't why I'm calling, though."

"Figured as much."

Linc got off the hard plastic chair and walked to the wall to look out the glass door. It overlooked paved walkways and manicured landscaping, all taken care of by a monthly fee that went with his lease.

He scrubbed at his jaw with his knuckles, over the stubble he hadn't bothered to shave. "I wondered what happened to that object I gave you."

"Nealy's job was to return it to her superiors in DC."

Linc's heart sped up. "So she's in DC?"

"Probably by now, yeah."

Fuck. Linc felt like a dumb ass for not thinking of it himself. He hadn't exactly been thinking straight — or at all last night.

The walls of the small space seemed to loom closer, so he pushed outside to draw some fresh air. As soon as he pulled a breath into his lungs, he felt better.

"Thanks for the info, buddy. I'll let you get back to your horses and your pretty little wife," Linc said.

"Hey, Linc, you all right?"

"Couldn't be better." He rang off and rubbed at his jaw.

Even if he didn't exactly feel it, his statement was true.

He wasn't trapped in a crate, he wasn't stuck in a hospital.

But he wasn't feeling himself either.

Stepping back inside, he saw the dryer was finished, so he walked over and stuffed all the warm clothes into the bag without bothering to fold them. Tossing it over his shoulder, he headed back home, making plans in his mind about how to shake off his ghosts. Even the good ones with plump lips and a dirty mouth.

Chapter Six

As Nealy stepped onto the elevator and the doors closed, she had a strong case of déjà vu. Different elevator in another building, and Linc wasn't here, but her mind—and body—had muscle memory, and she couldn't stop the feelings bombarding her system.

Leaving Linc's bed in the wee hours of the night to catch the red-eye to DC had been a bit of a turning point for her.

She'd gone from firmly disliking the man—he was cocky and pushy when it came to telling her what she should do—to fighting more than a few warm, fuzzy feelings toward him.

She had absolutely no business letting those thoughts into her brain. It had been sex—nothing more.

But as she rode up to the floor housing the ATF office, her heart was beating a bit too fast.

She couldn't believe the things she'd done with Linc—or demanded from him. That wasn't her. Or was it? Confused thoughts still whirled in her brain as she stepped out of the elevator.

As soon as she walked into the office, people called out greetings, and she responded with smiles and waves, though her focus was directed on getting the item she carried tucked so close to her body into the hands of her superiors. In this case, Mark Mitchum.

He was expecting her, sitting in his office with the door open. When she poked her head in, he said, "Close the door, Alexander."

She hadn't seen him in days, but was it her imagination that he looked somehow more put together? Maybe his increase of salary had afforded him a new wardrobe. The suit he wore was tailored to fit his form, and a gold watch she hadn't seen before flashed on his wrist as he held out a hand to shake.

"I heard you have good news for me," he said smoothly. "Please sit."

She did, feeling grubby in comparison after the flight and very little sleep. She smoothed a hand over her jeans and looked to her director.

Suddenly, she realized the big desk and the larger office with a window that overlooked the city had lost a bit of its luster for her. If she'd been promoted, she never would have been with Ranger Ops, in the field working to bring down Operation X firsthand.

And that had been the mother of adrenaline rushes. She could see why people got into the military now. Those commercials that said you could reach beyond your limits were true. She was a woman who was confident in her skills, but she'd never imagined in her life would she climb that cliff face to reach the mark, let alone all the events that followed.

He got up and closed the door, glancing around in the hall before he did so. When he returned to his desk and sat, he offered her a big smile. "You know, big things come to those who perform."

She studied him. "That's typically how the world operates, yes."

"Adding this to your file will make the right people sit up and take notice of you, Alexander."

She cocked her head. Why was he buttering her up? What was in it for him? Mitchum wasn't a man who handed out praise unless it made him shine too, which was probably the case with the flash drive. It was his victory as well.

He shot a look at the door, but nobody came through it.

"Are you expecting someone?" she asked.

"No." He leaned forward. "Do you have it?"

She gave a nod. "I wouldn't trust it to my luggage and I carried it all the way."

"And it was in the spot you were told?" He picked up his pen.

She hesitated. It was and it wasn't, but what were a few inches to the left? She'd probably seen that divot in the wallpapered wall and mistook it for the location, when it was really just a dent from a piece of furniture or something.

"Yes, it was there," she said.

Mitchum pushed out a breath. "Hand it over."

She nodded and slipped a hand into her jacket and a pocket inside a pocket where she'd stashed the flash drive. Mark watched her pull it free, and she placed it on the desk between them.

At first, he stared at it as if she'd just collected the Holy Grail, and then he reached across the desk and covered it with a hand. "Tell the Ranger Ops they did a good job, Alexander. You're dismissed."

She blinked at him. "The Ranger Ops?"

She waited for him to say more, but he didn't and all her anger rose up.

Was this asshole seriously giving them all the credit, when she'd been their reason for even going and without her, they wouldn't have known where to go, how to get in... so many details that she'd provided to them.

And they wouldn't have even gotten the flash drive if not for her. Sure, she hadn't punched through the wall like Linc had — *damn, that was hot* — but she'd been behind that too.

"Yes, you can give them my thanks and the accolades they deserve."

Fury rushed over her like a big black funnel cloud, about to whip her up into the frenzy she needed to cut off before she unleashed her storm of anger onto her boss.

She drew a deep breath and stuffed down her ire.

"Thanks again, Alexander." Mitchum bent his head toward the door.

She got to her feet, standing her ground. "That's it? We're not going to look at what's on the flash drive?"

Eyeing her, he said, "That's for further analysis by those with higher security clearances than you, Alexander." He shot a fake smile that fell flat on her. When he stood to dismiss her, she straightened her shoulders.

"Look—I deserve as much recognition for accomplishing this mission as Ranger Ops. I came off that cliff as soot-covered as any of the Ranger Ops team."

Mark gave her that same ingratiating smile. God, she wanted to punch it off his stupid, smug face. "You're getting your emotions tangled up in this, Alexander. Do I need to remove you from the case?"

His statement infuriated her more, and she forced her rage back like a genie stoppered into a bottle. With as much of an even tone as she could muster, she said, "My emotions have nothing to do with this." She held his gaze for more than a minute, and he stared right back in a battle of wills.

She was just beginning to think they might stand here all day, when the door opened behind her and Chief of Staff Holden entered. "Mitchum, did I just see the latest Lexus in your parking spot with your initials on the license plate? That thing's a beauty—" He rambled to a halt and looked between them, obviously catching the tension hovering thick in the air.

"A word, Mitchum," he said and looked to Nealy. "Alexander. A pat on the back's in order, I believe."

"Thank you, sir." She didn't feel as good about her achievement with Ranger Ops now that her douchebag of an acting deputy director had belittled her role in the mission and made that sexist remark that her emotions were involved. A common thing women in the ATF and all other government positions had faced at one time or other. People thought that because they were capable of love, motherhood and friendship, as well as bad-ass, hardcore brain-iac and physical strengths, that they were some kind of breed different from those who had dicks between their legs.

Well, she had news for them.

Suddenly, it wasn't lost on her that the Ranger Ops had all clapped her on the back along with the others after they'd made it off that cliff. They'd treated her as an equal, and that surprised her, when she'd expected them to be all macho and take the credit.

"Thank you, sir," Nealy managed to respond to Holden and gave Mitchum a final glare. "And you're welcome, Acting Deputy Director."

Turning on her heel, she headed out of the office, not even bothering to glance at her own cubicle space. She would not be sitting in it today—she was going home and take a hot shower and try to do something with the anger boiling inside her.

Too bad Linc's not around. We could fuck it out.

* * * * *

Linc crossed his legs on the porch railing and kicked back with his beer, looking over the sunset on Sully's ranch. The entire spread had been left to him and his wife Nevaeh after a good friend of his had died, a two-times widower with no family to speak of.

"I'll say it again, man. You're one lucky son of a bitch," Linc drawled.

Sully swigged his beer, relaxing in a similar pose, while his wife lay in a chair beside him, reading a book.

They hadn't gotten to ride for very long, but just being outdoors and getting some exercise with the animals he loved had given Linc a bit of the release he needed. He was still keyed up, though.

But that had to do with a sexy little ATF agent who'd stirred him up all over again. First the elevator and now the dirty shower scene that had blown his mind had him wanting more.

The fading rays of the sun were drawing lines through the sky in shades of yellow and orange.

"How's your momma?" Sully asked.

"She's ornery as ever. Complaining about the neighbors mowing parts of the land that belong to her, when Lennon and I tell her she should just let

97

them mow it and save her the work and gas for the tractor. And at the same time, she loves the same neighbors because they just foaled and she loves watching them."

Sully chuckled. "Sounds like she needs some grandbabies to keep her busy."

Linc sipped his beer, enjoying the local craft blend. "Well, Lennon needs to get on that."

"When was the last time you took a woman home to your momma?" he asked.

Linc snorted. "I mighta been about sixteen."

Nevaeh looked up from her book. "You haven't been serious about a woman since you were sixteen?"

Linc lowered his bottle from his lips. "Wasn't really serious about that one either."

They all laughed.

"What about that ATF agent?"

His neck popped as he whipped his head toward his buddy. "What would make you think about her?"

"Dude, I've seen you on how many missions now? I've never seen you hover over anyone the way you do her. All protective like." He shot a look at his wife, who was giving him a soft smile. "Been there before."

Nevaeh reached over and touched Sully's hand.

Linc pushed to his feet. "Time for me to head on home. Good thing I didn't have that third beer."

Sully stood too. "So you don't really care that Agent Alexander is back in town and staying at the Marriot?"

Linc felt a jerk in his gut, like someone had just hooked him and given it a yank. Damn... He couldn't let his captain see his interest, though.

Stretching, Linc said, "Why would I care about that?"

Sully chuckled. "Suit yourself, Linc. Thanks for comin' by."

"Enjoyed myself. Thank you for being a gracious and lovely host, Nevaeh." He took her hand and squeezed. "See you for bowling tomorrow night if we don't have other obligations."

"I'll look forward to it, Linc," Nevaeh said.

"I'll see myself out." He took his leave, and as he headed out to his car, his mind — and body — were very aware of what Sully had told him. Nealy was miles away, and he could be spreading her thighs within the hour.

Biting off a growl, he reached the crossroads. He drew to a stop and looked right and then left.

Go to her, his body urged.

Don't fuck with her more than you already have, his mind directed.

The sun was sinking quickly. He had all night ahead of him, alone, and he didn't have to be.

But what could he offer Nealy? He sure wasn't taking her home to his momma. What would he say

99

when he introduced her — this woman drove me crazy for a month when I was at my worst in the hospital after being imprisoned in a crate for days... then I fucked her in an elevator and all that changed?

But *had* all that changed?

He gripped the wheel and stared straight ahead at the land, the sky and the fading daylight. Yeah, it had changed, but it wasn't the sex that'd flipped the switch in his brain. He didn't know quite *what* it was.

Decision made, he turned left, away from the hotel and Nealy.

* * * * *

Nealy's contacts weren't dried out and playing tricks on her. She gently rubbed at her eyes just to be certain, but sure enough, when she opened her eyes, the same words were on the screen of her computer tablet.

Hot damn.

Her superiors had to know about this. She really had just unearthed a bit of information that was dire to the Operation X case.

But who to share it with? Her immediate boss was Mitchum, but after the way he'd dismissed her role in getting the flash drive, she didn't care much to speak to the man.

What other choice did she have? Going above him would only get her in trouble and below him could mean information leaked into the hands of someone who wasn't cleared to know.

She pushed out a sigh and pulled her tablet closer. Cradling it, she took a screenshot and forwarded it using an encrypted, encoded and password-protected connection.

Okay, now her contacts were actually drying out. When she stood from the hard hotel chair and made her way to the bathroom, her body screamed at her for holding it in the same position for too long. She'd gone from Linc's bed to an airplane seat, the ATF office, home where she'd pored over files all night, before she finally decided the only way to continue making progress on the Operation X case was to team up with the Ranger Ops again.

Which meant yet another flight and here she was going over yet more new and breaking details in the case.

She removed her contacts and did what every beauty expert warned her against and rubbed her eyes. To hell with wrinkles.

She splashed her face with cold water and put on her glasses. After she returned to the hotel seating and picked up her tablet, she saw she'd missed a message in all caps—CALLING YOU.

Her phone buzzed and she brought it to her ear. "Alexander."

"What the hell do you think you're doing, Alexander?"

Just hearing Mitchum's voice made her jaws snap together. "What are you talking about?" she bit off.

"You're digging into things that are way above your level." He let out a bark of a laugh.

"Then why is it Homeland has given me access?" She felt her body coil up with the shot of adrenaline to her system.

"As your director, I advise you to stop looking and allow us to feed you the information necessary to do your job, agent. You don't know what sort of trouble you just got me in by sending that screenshot just now."

She took a deep breath. Could that be true?

Even if it was, she wasn't going to bow down to this man. "Just doing what I was asked to do, Mitchum. If you've got a problem with it, I suggest you ask the director of Homeland Security why he provided me with the access key. Goodnight, Mitchum."

Hanging up and getting the last word should make her feel good, but it was far from the truth. Her hands were a little shaky and she felt as if she'd just gotten into a sparring match with a man holding a knife. It was obvious Mitchum was out for her blood, but she could only think it was because she posed a threat to him. She was next in line for his position, and if he messed up…

She strode back to the bathroom, brushed her teeth and turned off the lights and flopped into bed.

It wasn't as comfy as her own back in DC or Linc's, just twenty minutes away.

She stared up at the ceiling for long minutes. Some of her anger had just burned off, when her room phone rang, shooting the adrenaline through her body all over again.

If this was Mitchum, she was going to throw the phone off the balcony.

When she answered and heard the gritty, deep baritone of Linc's voice in her ear, her insides froze.

"Nealy. I've... got a problem."

"Linc, what's wrong? Where are you?"

"Home. I'm just... having an episode or something."

Oh God.

Her heartrate rocketed through the atmosphere and shot across the sky like a meteor. She jerked upright and perched on the edge of the bed. "What kind of episode? What's your address? I missed it when I was there the other night."

"I don't know what's wrong. I'm just... not right. Can you come?"

The plea didn't just tug her heartstrings—it ripped them right out of her chest. This big, rough Ranger Ops guy was asking her for help.

She got the address, grabbed her purse and ran out of the hotel. Outside, she managed to get an Uber and while she sat in the cramped back seat, she clenched and unclenched her fists on her lap. She cracked all her knuckles, which earned her a glance from the driver.

Her mind raced over scenarios. An episode? Was Linc depressed and facing down dark thoughts? She'd heard her share of sad stories with tragic endings.

Maybe he was ill—an infection from his burns or even some aftereffects of the explosion they'd all lived through in Chihuahua. He had been closer to the blast, sheltering her with his body...

The miles didn't go by fast enough, and she was really losing it by the time the driver pulled up in front of the security gates. She told him what apartment to call, and he did. A second later, when Linc buzzed them through, relief made her cheeks and lips tingle.

He still had enough faculties to allow her in.

She hopped out and quickly paid the driver, and then she ran up to Linc's front door.

She knocked, and he called out, "It's open."

As soon as she stepped inside, she felt the charge in the air. Then she set eyes on Linc, sitting in a leather armchair, elbows on his knees and head in his hands. She let out a rasp of relief.

"What's happened?" She rushed over to him and hit her knees, staring at him.

When he suddenly jumped to his feet, she was forced backward, where she sat on her haunches, watching him pace the dark room.

He wheeled around, not looking at her, and went to the window. The stiffness in the set of his shoulders urged her to stand, and she went to him. Wrapping her arms around him from behind, she released a low sigh at touching him again.

"Linc." She tried to turn him in her arms, but he didn't budge. "Talk to me."

"It's dumb. I'm dumb. It's just all coming back to me, the walls are so close and... Fuck, I hated it. Hated *them*. I want to take them out, every goddamn last man who is part of that group."

A shiver ran through her. Realizing he wouldn't turn to her, she slipped around him, between his big body and the window he was staring blankly out.

"Linc." She cupped his face, tracing the hard features on his face with her gaze. A muscle fluttered in his jaw. "Linc, you'll get them. *We'll* get them. I came back, because I can't let it go either, and together we'll see it through to the end. Can I get you some water? Maybe something stronger to take the edge off?"

He let out a low breath and dropped his gaze to her. The instant their eyes met, something changed in him.

A fierce expression burned over his face as he leaned in and slammed his mouth over hers.

The taste of man and desire struck her full force, and she clung to his neck even as he lifted her and turned for his room.

An unsettled force took hold low in her belly, and she wrapped her thighs around his waist and rubbed against his front.

He issued a growl and kicked open the door to his room. The bed was a shadowed shape in the darkness, but he navigated to it in a step or two and laid her down on the neatly made mattress.

"I knew you'd come," he whispered.

"I couldn't have stayed away, Linc."

"Let me have you—all of you, babe. I need you."

She stared into his eyes, glittering with lust. "I'm yours."

And she was—not because he asked but because she wanted to give herself—she wanted him just as badly.

Leaning up on her elbows, she captured his mouth again in a long, deep, tongue- tangling kiss that spiraled on for so long that she lost track of time. It might be midnight or three a.m. All she knew were the flavors he filled her head with and the low rumble coming from his chest as he slanted his mouth over hers with more and more insistence.

She reached for his shirt and pulled it over his head. Until that moment when she touched hard, velvety steel, she hadn't realized just how damn much she'd missed Linc.

Drawing lines with her fingertips up and down his back was total pleasure for her. When he reared back to look into her eyes, the universe faded, leaving only the two of them.

He tore off her clothes, and she went for his jeans. They tumbled over and over on the covers, until he poised at the root of her, his hard shaft solid between her legs.

"Take me," she rasped.

He claimed her in one hard thrust. Stretching her inner walls, pulling a cry from her lips as he braced his muscular arms around her and began to thrust. The fire in his eyes built. Her insides flexed around him, and he jerked his hips upward.

Clinging to his broad shoulders, she bucked against him, spearing herself with every sharp plunge he gave. The bed shook, and her mind emptied of anything but the haze of bliss.

"There. Right there!"

He dipped into her again. "Here?"

"Yesss." She caught his lower lip between her teeth, tugging him down for a kiss as her world melted with an explosive orgasm.

He watched her come apart for him, gaze burning down at her. When she regained her wits enough to take charge, she did, pushing on him until he fell onto the mattress. She slung her leg over his hips and took his length right into her pussy in one slick glide.

A groan left his lips. Feeling heady with power, she pushed onto her knees, withdrawing on all ten inches of him. Not that she'd measured, but whatever his length, it felt damn impressive.

Reaching up, he cupped her bare breasts, strumming her nipples with his thumbs and tormenting her until she was right on the cusp of coming again.

"Hold on." He gripped her hips hard, keeping her from moving more.

Her hair fell around her face, and she shook it away to look into his eyes. "What is it?"

"Promise me something."

"What?"

"You won't get up and leave in the night."

Her heart somersaulted, flipping in a way she'd never experienced before, and that was saying something about the way she was beginning to feel about Linc.

Easing forward, she held his gaze. "I won't leave," she whispered.

His grip on her changed, and he lifted her off his cock. She felt herself moving up the mattress and then his wet tongue sinking into her folds.

Oh no, she wasn't leaving this bed, this man, anytime soon.

*****

Linc had kicked himself a dozen times after calling Nealy and telling her he needed her. The bad-ass-never-say-die part of himself wasn't happy that he'd shown any vulnerability.

But with her in his arms, he felt more powerful and in control than he had all night.

The memories plaguing him faded, leaving only raw desire and the taste of her sweet pussy on his lips.

He thumbed her outer lips apart and sucked on her juicy clit. She rocked on his tongue, and he sank a finger into her sheath. Then two. And added a third, spreading her wide open for him.

She went wild, tossing her head and crying out, shaking against his mouth as a massive release struck. Her cum soaked his fingers that he pumped into her in time to the sucking pulls of his mouth. His cock stood straight up at the musky taste of her on his lips, and he couldn't hold back another second from filling her with his cock.

His cum.

She hung forward, panting, and he flipped her again, cradling her ass with one palm, and yanked her up and onto him. He slid home with a grunt and began to move.

Fucking her hard and deep, his mind galloping faster than he'd driven Sully's horse on earlier. The head of his cock hit the perfect sweet spot, and he stiffened as the tingle of ecstasy started at the base of his spine.

He sank into her five times... six.

His bellow echoed off the walls, and the enormous spurt of cum had to fill her entire pussy. On the second, she overflowed, and he reached down to catch a bead of their combined fluid on his fingertip and fed it to her.

She parted her lips for a taste, eyes glazed and shiny with lust as he pumped out the final bit of his release.

Seconds later, he found her snuggled into the crook of his neck, her damp body plastered against his.

He enveloped her hand in his and closed his eyes, feeling calm at last.

"Linc…"

"Hm?"

"What the hell was that?"

A laugh bubbled up from him, unexpected and freeing at the same time. "That, babe, was the best sex you've ever had."

"What about you? Was it the best sex you've had?"

"Hands fucking down."

She tipped her head, and he caught the smug smile spreading over her beautiful face. He couldn't believe he'd ever thought her plain. After looking closer, what he saw was a woman meant for him and him alone.

He pinched her backside, and she let out a small squawk.

"You were coming to me anyway," he said.

She nodded. "I was. We've got lots of work to do."

He pinched her harder, and this time she batted his hand away. "Work can wait. We only have one 'now.'"

Her eyes grew serious. "We can make a lot more nows."

God, she was gorgeous, and he couldn't get enough of her. He cupped her face and studied her eyes. "Is that what you want?" His voice took on a gritty edge.

She nodded, but when she leaned into his hand, the action solidified her answer in his mind.

In his heart.

Chapter Seven

Linc balanced the tray on one hand and smoothed the other over Nealy's shoulder and down the length of one bare arm. It took her a moment to rouse from sleep, but when she opened her eyes, he smiled at her.

"Mm. Is that eggs I smell?"

"Yes. I cooked you breakfast."

"Will you be sharing it with me in bed?" she mumbled, still in the clutches of sleep.

He sighed. "I've gotta head out, babe. But I wanted to wake you to say goodbye."

She rocketed into a sitting position, eyes wide now as she took in his black cargo pants and T-shirt. The rest of his gear was waiting for him—and so was the Ranger Ops SUV.

"What do you mean you're heading out? Where?"

"I can't tell you that." The corner of his mouth tipped into a soft smile. He placed the tray on the bed next to her. "I didn't know what kind of jam you liked, but I only had two, so I gave you one slice of toast with each."

She didn't even glance at the food, which he knew she wouldn't. "You're not telling me what's going on and you're leaving right now?"

"I have to," he responded, feeling a little tug of the separation that awaited them. He never knew when he'd return.

Or if.

No, he'd come back from that fucking truck with pig shit and the crate. Not only did he need to fulfill his promise to see his momma soon but he had to finish what he started with Nealy. What exactly that entailed, he hadn't quite figured out yet, but he would.

"Take me with you." She threw back the sheet covering her nudity. At the sight of her warm, freckled skin, his cock surged.

"Babe, you can't."

"Is it Operation X?"

"No." He got a slight pang at the bald-faced lie, but he didn't want her in this shit. Sully hadn't told him Nealy was to be part of it either.

His voice came out gruffer, because dammit, he was feeling emotions that had no business in the life of a man like him.

"You're keeping me in the dark because I'm female."

He chuckled. "Why would you think that? You know I have hardcore respect for what you did with us back at the cliffs. Now, eat your breakfast. Hang out here and work if you need to. There's no point in you staying at the hotel if my bed is open."

She eyed him, severe mistrust on her face. "Are you keeping me out of this because we slept together?"

That was part of it, but no way was he telling her that either.

"Nealy," he said gently, taking her nipple between finger and thumb and easing her back against the pillow with his lips on hers. She sighed against his mouth but succumbed to his kiss.

"At least tell me you'll follow the rules so you don't get yourself in more trouble," she whispered.

"I don't always follow the rules, if it means I get what I want." He arched a brow at her.

"You're too rebel for me, and that's what I don't like about you."

"I think the rebel in me is exactly what you like about me." He slipped his hand down her body, between her thighs. The damp warmth of her almost made him groan out loud, but this was about her and leaving her with a smile on her face.

She opened her mouth to argue her point again, when he thrust his fingers inside her pussy. She cried out, words dying on her lips. Stretching his pinky down over the seam between pussy and ass, he found her tight little pucker and sank his finger into her backside.

Twisting on the bed, she said, "Linc!"

114

He settled his thumb over her clit and drew circles over it as he finger-banged her. Watching her writhe, her nipples tightening into hard gumdrops, and the way she bit at her lower lip, plumping it up even more, had him rock-hard.

But he didn't have time to take away more than this moment—her cries, her flush of pleasure and the scent of her on his hand when he left.

She trembled, belly dipping and breasts rising with her sharp breaths. When he angled his hand and breached her another millimeter, she went dead still. Her stare on his, her eyes alight with something he could only guess at.

And hope for.

He brought her over the edge. Her pussy tightened on his hand, her ass clenched and her clit hardened into a pearl as he stroked her into the final frenzy.

She collapsed on the bed, and he leaned in to kiss her long and deep before pulling his fingers free and standing.

"I'll see you when I get back," he said.

"You can't just leave after that."

"I have to live up to my reputation of being a rebel. Your eggs are gettin' cold, babe." With a supreme amount of willpower, he walked out.

* * * * *

What... the fuck... was that? Nealy heard the front door close and knew Linc had gone. Still breathing hard, she glanced over at the plate sitting on the bed. It looked like the man could cook a decent breakfast.

And turn her into a puddle of desire in seconds. Her body still thrummed from the after effects of her orgasm. She reached for the plate. The eggs were already cold, so she just nibbled the toast, amused that he had given her two types of jam because he didn't know her preference.

Funny thing was, she knew just as little about him.

Except how he looked as the last jet of cum pumped into her body.

She swung her legs out of bed and looked around for her clothes. She found something more comfortable—Linc's shirt still crumpled on the floor. She picked it up and brought it to her nose automatically, catching a whiff of his musky scent on the cloth.

Which sent her body into overdrive all over again.

She had to think about this rationally.

He revved her libido, that much was obvious. But she'd also realized he wasn't the man she thought him to be, back in their hospital visit days when he clearly disliked her and she thought he was all testosterone and few brains.

Now, she was embarrassed she'd even thought those things, but she knew he held similar opinions at one time.

She was also humbled that at his low point, he'd called her to come over. Just him asking for her had her melting for him more.

Then he'd pulled his macho act this morning, showing her who was boss in his bed.

She grinned and slipped his shirt over her head. It hung loose on her frame and hit her midthigh, but she felt like a princess in it.

Grabbing the plate, she strode to the kitchen. There she was stunned to find not a single dirty dish in the sink, as she'd expected from any man. She scraped her plate into the trash and looked into the dishwasher. There were the rest of the dirty dishes and he even had the detergent ready. She liked a man who cleaned up after himself. She stowed the dish inside and hit the start button.

With a look around, she saw the whole apartment in a similar state of neatness. Mail stacked in a way that was almost OCD, with the corners lined up perfectly. The pillows on the sofa were plumped and lined along the back. And his boots were even neatly placed side-by-side at the door. A cowboy hat hung on coat rack above the shoes, and too easily she could picture it tugged low over his eyes as he squinted into the sunset.

With nothing to do, she had only herself to worry about. He was gone and wanted her to stay here, but all her things were at the hotel.

She took a quick shower—using his body wash had her pussy clenching all over again—and she dressed in the clothes she'd arrived in. She couldn't find a spare toothbrush, so she rinsed with mouthwash. After that, she called for a ride.

On the way to the hotel, Mark phoned. She brought the cell to her ear, aware of the driver inches away and how she would avoid any sensitive topics.

As soon as she answered, Mark spoke. "Alexander. Tell Ranger Ops that the rally point for Nuevo Leon is—"

"Wait. I'm not with them and have no way of getting ahold of them." She darted a look at the driver, who seemed not to be paying attention, but she couldn't take any chances.

A beat of silence. Then Mark exploded in her ear.

"What the hell do you mean you aren't with them? This information came down from our office—and you're not even with the team? I always took you as an agent who slides by and lets other people do the work, but this is fucking ridiculous, Alexander. You had one job and that is to stick with Ranger Ops until Operation X is buried in the ground. This could mean your badge, Alexander. Are you following me now? I didn't send you to Texas to get a spot of sun!"

"I wasn't informed they were going. I'll take care of it and catch up to them."

"There's no way in hell that's happening. They're in the fucking chopper, and since you're not on it, you aren't going. Are you working on your tan by the hotel pool? This is our chance to prove how the ATF can work together with Homeland Security as equals, and now you've cost us the entire operation."

Anger rose up, strong and bright, tasting like copper on her tongue. She pitched her voice low and steady as she said, "I will fix it, Mark."

Before he could go off at her anymore, she ended the call. The strong burst of adrenaline from being told off had her heart thumping hard.

She didn't know who she was more pissed at— her director or her lover.

Linc had knowingly gone without her.

Left her behind on a mission he knew she needed to be part of. She balled her fist on her thigh and restrained her need to throw back her head and bellow her frustration.

She thought they were a team, that she'd proved herself to him and the rest of Ranger Ops. Clearly, she was mistaken. They viewed her as a hindrance, maybe even a liability.

And her job was on the line. Mark had made that *damn* clear.

She had to get to the hotel and find a way to contact Linc. She knew the unit wasn't allowed personal cell phones in the event they were captured, as Linc had been. But they still had other communication, and she was damn well going to be heard.

Giving herself a good kick was in order as well. She'd let down her guard, been unprofessional. Mark wasn't far off base when he said he hadn't sent her to Texas for pleasure, and wasn't that exactly what she'd gotten all night in Linc's bed? And this morning, when she should have been questioning him about where he was headed, she'd been lying back, enjoying his thick fingers buried in her pussy.

A growl of frustration left her, and the driver glanced back. "Everything okay?"

God, she also needed her own rental car. She couldn't deal with nosy drivers.

"Fine," she murmured and looked out the window as the city crawled by at what seemed like a snail's pace when she needed to be sprinting like a roadrunner.

When she finally reached the hotel room, she walked straight to her tablet and logged in to the restricted database. It took only a few minutes to get a number locked into her mind, and she punched it in to her cell.

"Reed."

"Linc," she said.

"No, Lennon. But I can be Linc if you need me to be."

She pushed out a breath and jammed her fingers into her loose hair. "I don't have time to play the game of guess-the-right-twin. But maybe it's better if I don't speak to *that man* right now. Lennon, I need your coordinates so I can meet up with you."

"Uh... negative. I am not at liberty to discuss it."

"Lennon, cut the shit. I need to get to Nuevo Leon and help you take out that cell." Her jaw ached from withholding a scream.

"No can do, Alexander. We'll speak to you when we get back."

The line went dead.

* * * * *

Linc whipped his head toward his twin, the name echoing in his skull and reverberating throughout his entire body along with the whir of the chopper blades not twenty feet from their team.

"Alexander?" Each boot he laid down between him and his twin felt like a thud of an earthquake.

Why the fuck had Lennon been talking to Nealy? Better yet, how the fuck had she found a way to contact the team?

Lennon shot him a look. "Dude, get hold of yourself. No need to look like you're going for the throat. I told her she can't be part of this."

"Goddammit, she wasn't even supposed to know!"

"Which is odd to me because she knew exactly where we're headed. Clearly, somebody told her she needed to go along." Lennon narrowed his eyes.

"She didn't need to come, no matter what her orders were."

"Wait a minute, bro." Lennon cocked his head and widened his stance. "Agent Alexander was *supposed to* be here with us and you stepped over those orders and made your own choice not to inform her?"

Linc glared at his interfering twin. "Sully never said she was supposed to join us, so I didn't tell her. Like I said, we got this. She's not needed."

"It's because you're in love with her."

Linc grabbed his brother by the arms and stared into his eyes. Lennon's words cut across him like the slash of a Bowie knife.

Fuck, now what?

He released Lennon and spun away.

His brother caught up to him, jogging to keep up to Linc's pace. "C'mon, man. Say it. Do you love her?"

"Fuck off."

"All you gotta do is admit it to me and I'll leave you alone about it."

"Get the fuck away from me."

The chopper blades cut through the air as it lifted off, leaving Ranger Ops on the ground and fending for themselves.

"Say it, Linc," Lennon wheedled like they were ten and he was asking his twin if he liked a girl in the fourth grade.

"Get the hell away from me."

"All you have to do is say five little words — yes, I love her, Lennon. Or bro. You could say bro instead of my full name. I — "

Linc stopped walking and made a move to ram him off his feet.

"Hey, hey, hey!" Sully and Shaw were there, arms thrown out to create a barricade between them.

An arm came like a hard steel band around Linc's chest as Shaw attempted to hold him back. Lennon shot him a shit-eating grin that had Linc's fists curling.

"Just say it, man. Say you love her," Lennon said.

"Fuck yes!" The cords of his neck strained with the yell.

"You what? You said you love her?"

Linc tore free of Shaw's hold and strode away. "Ask me one more time and I'll put a bullet in you."

His twin's laugh followed him, along with a few other chuckles. But Linc didn't think it was one bit funny that he'd fallen in love with Nealy, a woman he hadn't liked from the beginning.

But she grew on me.

And who was probably right now seething after finding out that he'd kept her from joining them to stop a shipment of semi-autos about to hit the highway and cross the border in one of their trucks filled with pig shit.

The memory of the scent burned his brain, resurrecting the claustrophobic feeling he was determined to beat.

She has no business anywhere near it.

Because I love her.

* * * * *

The wind from the chopper blades blew a tendril of Nealy's hair free from her severe ponytail and across her face. She reached up to direct it behind her ear, but it refused to stay. Ignoring it, she watched as the chopper door opened and a big, bulky man jumped to the ground. Followed by another and another.

They spotted her standing there, arms folded and her best don't-fuck-with-me expression. Of course, Linc was the last to get out of the helicopter, and by this time, she'd perfected her glare.

His boots hit the asphalt, and he glanced up. From this distance, she couldn't see much more than a tightening of his lips.

How could he have done this to her? Her job was on the line and he'd screwed with her career, her livelihood. She wasn't going to be stuck in some corner cubicle desk job for the rest of her days.

When he began to approach, she stiffened. To think this man had made her feel all warm and fuzzy after he left her yesterday. She was only angrier with herself for letting down her guard, allowing a man to sweet-talk her—or finger-bang her—into believing what they had was something deeper.

Silly, stupid and reckless, when her job was at stake. She'd already lost to Mark Mitchum and now another man was undermining her position.

"Happy to see me, I gather," Linc said above the whir of the chopper.

She shifted her weight to the other foot. Her arms were so tense that the muscles were beginning to lock up.

"It's a joke, babe."

"Don't babe me," she snapped. "You know exactly what you did to me, Reed."

"So I'm back to Reed. Okay, Alexander, what exactly did I do to you?" He caught her by the arm and whirled her around to keep pace with him as he made his way from the chopper that was lifting off and the rest of the Ranger Ops team, looking on.

She yanked from Linc's grasp and strode out ahead of him, blocking his path and forcing him to confront her. They were having this out, and he wasn't taking the coward's path and dodging her wrath.

He took one look at her face and bit off, "Not here, Nealy."

125

"Well, if you think I'm getting into a car with you, you're fucking crazy. After I tell you just how much you screwed me over, I'm getting in my car and driving far away from you." She didn't want to admit how much it hurt her to say those words, but it was for the best. Whatever they had was over now, and she would get back to her life.

Without Linc.

His brows pinched, and for a second, she saw the same mask of pain that he'd exposed to her after he'd called for her to come to him. He stopped walking and looked into her eyes. "Please, Nealy. Just come with me."

Damn that harsh, gritty tone of his. It lured her in every time.

Pushing out a breath, she gave a single nod. She'd hear him out, but she wouldn't be taken in by whatever he had to say. She would make up her own mind about his actions and how they affected her, and not be sucked into any of his excuses.

"You good, guys?" Sully called out to them.

Linc lifted a hand and waved. Nealy led him to the rental car she'd driven and got behind the wheel. She was in the driver's seat in this game — in all ways.

He crowded into the economy car's passenger seat, his neck bent so his head wasn't smashed against the ceiling. "Could you get a smaller car?" he asked.

"All they had at the last minute. I guess there's some convention in town."

Mundane talk between people who'd shared a lot more. She swallowed and opened her mouth to speak.

Before a word expelled, Linc said, "I know you're pissed."

"Pissed doesn't begin to cover it, Linc."

He ran a hand over his face, and she saw how tired he was. Also, his knuckles sported several cuts as if he'd been in a brawl. She couldn't imagine what he'd dealt with, but dammit, she should have been there with him.

"I'm not some shivering princess, you know. I was trained to handle extreme situations. I was responsible for taking out Manilo, the huge drug lord in Miami. I don't mean from behind a desk, sending guns in to do my dirty work. I mean, I faced him, Linc. And I made a kill shot because he forced me to it when he had me in his sights."

He let out a low groan. "Jesus, Nealy. I can't stand to think of you in danger like that."

His statement tripped her up. Her heart was beating faster, but she didn't want to react to his sweetness, his concern. She wanted him to see her for the strong, deadly woman she could be when the situation called for it.

"You put me in a bad situation. My acting deputy director's holding my job over my head now. Threatening to rip my position out from under my feet and leave me with nothing but a crap desk job processing paperwork. I was supposed to be with Ranger Ops, and you kept me from going. Why? How could you do that?" Her voice raised a notch with her renewed fury.

"You're right—I shouldn't have lied to you."

"Damn straight you shouldn't have!"

"But if I'm guilty of living up to my oath to protect and serve, then so be it."

She stared at him. "Do you think you need to protect me?" She released a short laugh.

His direct gaze burned into her, his eyes burning with intensity. "Yes, I fucking do, Nealy. I fucking love you."

Her jaw dropped. Not a single breath passed through her lungs. When she started to see stars, she sucked in sharply, and oxygen flooded her brain. With it came his words, hitting her full force.

"You love me," she repeated.

God, could he be serious? She searched his face for a trace of humor but saw none. He was as serious as a heart attack, which she might have any moment.

She took another breath.

"Babe, I hated you at first. But now I see it for what it was—passion. A gut reaction to something that scared the balls off me."

"You're exhausted, haven't slept."

He shook his head. "That's not why I'm saying these things, and you know it, Nealy."

Hell, now what? Did he expect her to reply that she loved him too? She couldn't do that, because she had no idea where her feelings stood among the lust, pleasure, irritation and anger directed toward this man.

"Fuck, don't look at me that way. Do you think this is easy for me? Look at me. I'm six-two and two hundred and ten pounds. I carry a sniper rifle for a living and here I am gushing out cupid shit for a woman I'm pretty sure hates my guts."

Her stomach jerked as if she'd been dealt a blow. "I don't hate you, Linc," she said faintly.

"I made a mistake not telling you about the mission. But the idea of you in the thick of the shit we were about to face..." He shook his head. "I wanted to keep you out of it. I wanted to keep you safe, babe."

Her throat closed off, and she fought against her rising emotions on the tide of her extreme anger and the urge to smack his handsome face—right after brushing her fingertips over his rough stubble lining his chiseled jaw.

"Shit, Linc. Why did you have to say these things to me?" Dropping her head into her hand, she shook it back and forth.

"Damn. Do you want me to leave? The other guys haven't left yet."

She stared at the blank dashboard, mind in a fit of indecision. The professional part of herself wanted nothing to do with a man who was so determined to end her career. But the feminine part had tingles running through her entire system, and she wanted nothing more than to land in the lap of the man who'd just confessed his love to her.

She just wasn't sure if she could trust him after what he'd done, keeping her from the mission she was meant to be on. And if she couldn't trust in that, how could she believe anything else?

* * * * *

Linc sat in the dinky car seat with his knees up to his chin and his head cranked to the right, but he'd endure this for a week if it meant Nealy would give him a chance. He saw the headlights of the SUV pan across the parking lot as his team left without him.

"When I left this morning, I didn't know you were supposed to be with us. Sully didn't say anything to me."

She eyed him.

"The team just left, so either I'm walking or you're driving," he said quietly to Nealy.

Her chest rose and fell. Finally, she turned on the engine and rolled out of the parking lot. He wasn't certain what her destination might be. She could be taking him to her hotel, to his place or kicking him out into a ditch.

He probably deserved the latter—but dammit, even if Sully had told him she was meant to join them, Linc might have kept her from it, to protect her. Didn't she see that? Of course she had her job security weighing on her mind.

And she'd looked as if she'd been caught with her pants down when he told her he loved her.

Probably shouldn't have spilled that either. He was just making *all* the right choices with Nealy, wasn't he?

The car dinged, alerting him he wasn't wearing his seatbelt. She sliced a look at him.

"I can't buckle it. It's crowded in here."

She nodded and drove on. After a couple minutes, she shot him another glance from the corner of her eye. "Are you at least going to tell me about the mission?

"Technically, it's all classified information," he began.

She gave him a glare that would chill the balls off the devil.

"But I'll tell you anything you want to know," he finished.

"I'm listening," was all she said.

As she drove, he talked, giving her all the dirty details leading up to finding the men behind the weapons buried beneath tons of pig shit on their way across the border. But when he got to the part about not a single man being around, she hit the brakes and looked at him.

"What do you mean there was nobody around?"

131

"The trucks were abandoned. We searched the area, spread out over half a mile, but they were tipped off. Long gone."

"What the hell?"

"It happens. We find ways of luring them back."

"Such as?" She eyed him and continued to drive once more.

He grinned. "We blew up one of their trucks. Losing half a million dollars' worth of weapons brought them back in a hurry."

"Oh my God, Linc. You know my position is to investigate explosives too. Do I need to be concerned with the amount of explosives used by Ranger Ops?"

"Yes. Be very afraid." His grin widened, and for a moment she looked as if she might return it, but she turned her head aside and stared out the windshield again.

"So you blew the truck and they came running back. I'm assuming there was a fight."

He wasn't about to linger over the details of hand-to-hand combat and sprays of machine gun fire. Or the second rush of men they hadn't expected. Recalling those things made Linc glad Nealy had been kept out of it. He wouldn't have been able to fight *and* keep an eye on her.

Though it sounded as if she could handle herself. *Fucking Manilo.* He shook his head.

He gave her enough of a story to satisfy her curiosity. Then she went dead silent. He didn't know what to think of that or if he should say something to breach the silence. When she turned into his gated apartment complex and punched in his entry code, he stared at her.

"How'd you get access to that?"

She offered him a small smile. "You're not the only one with information. I also know you're withholding parts of the story you just told." She pulled into his driveway and parked the car.

He was given a look at her backside as she climbed out of the car. It took him a moment to unfold himself from the origami shape he'd settled into, then he followed her up to the apartment.

To his surprise, she also had his entry code to the front door. He was just about to give a smug snort because she wouldn't have a key to the deadbolt he'd installed after moving in. But she produced a gold key and stuck it into the lock.

"Jesus," he muttered.

She turned and shot him a grin. She pushed inside and flipped on a light. As soon as the warm glow illuminated her beautiful face, his heart shoved against his ribs.

He reached for her. "Nealy."

"Don't try to butter me up, Reed."

"If you don't want buttered up, why did you come home with me?" He cupped her face.

Her eyes slipped closed, and she let out a stuttering breath... and leaned into his touch.

"God, babe. C'mere." Unable to hold back another second, he pulled her into his arms. She was stiff at first, her arms enfolded against her body as a barrier between them. But when he buried his nose in her hair and breathed her in, she began to relax.

Inching his lips to her ear, he flicked his tongue over her soft earlobe. "I want to keep you safe."

She swallowed audibly.

He tongued the shell of her ear. "You can't blame me for loving you."

With a gasp, she threw her arms around his neck, a hand on his nape, and jerked him in for a kiss. The crush of her lips under his ripped a groan from him, and he lifted her against him, locked in his embrace as he plundered her mouth.

At that minute, it didn't matter that she hadn't returned his sentiment. It was enough that she knew how he felt.

It was enough that she was here with him and he might find a way to make everything up to her.

Chapter Eight

"How did you get my access code?" he whispered between rough, straining kisses.

The pulse thrumming through Nealy couldn't get more forceful — it was like the drums of war. And she didn't know if this was love or a fight to the finish. All she knew was neither were coming out of this without feeling the effects of the other.

Raking her nails over his spine, she reveled in his sharp intake of air. "Do you think you're the only one with insider perks?"

"I'll show you some inside perks." He cupped her ass, lifting her against his heavy erection. She wrapped her thighs around his waist and clung to his neck as he moved through the apartment to his bedroom.

The bed was neat, as she'd left it. And when he laid her down on the mattress, their mingled scents rose up to welcome her.

Linc braced his arms around her, doing a slow, grinding pushup against her body. Nuzzling his nose over hers, he moved down to her cleavage and then drew a line back up to deliver a toe-curling, tongue-tangling kiss.

She went for his clothes, and he went for hers. The untamed movements spoke of how much they wanted this. What she didn't know was why. Practically from the start, they'd been stalking each other in circles and now they couldn't keep their hands off each other. The sexual tension was off the charts.

He'd told her he loved her.

And God help her, she loved him too.

Yanking him down, she spread her legs and angled her bare pussy upward just as he thrust home. Seated deep, he gave her a dark look and ground his hips. The tip of his cock hit her innermost point, raising a cry from her throat.

"Linc. Fuck me."

"I'll do better than that. I'll make love to you."

Her heart shattered with love in return, though she couldn't vocalize it yet. She wasn't ready. She was still mad at him.

Wasn't she?

He palmed her breast and leaned in to suck on her throat, while she writhed against him. A twitch of her hips dislodged him enough that he withdrew an inch from her pussy. It felt so good, they both issued a groan and he began to fuck her the way she wanted to be fucked.

Deep, hard.

She took his lower lip between her teeth and tugged. Suddenly, she was tumbling as he flipped her to straddle him.

"I know you want to go at me. So here I am." He egged her on with a flash of white teeth.

"I'll take that challenge." She clenched her pussy around him as she sank to the hilt. Then she clamped her hands on his and locked them to the bed. Her hair hung around them, and she shook it back to give him a grin. "I'm going to drive you so crazy that you beg me to get you off."

She pulled off his cock again, this time teasing her wet folds over the mushroomed tip of him. Linc's eyes darkened as he stared up at her, his lust raw and exciting as hell.

Her insides fluttered, and he let out a growl.

"Don't make me flip you over and take you the way I want you," he said.

Sinking over his length, she pulled another rasp from him. She sat there, unmoving, until the muscle in the crease of his jaw began to twitch from restraint. She let the desire build, aching to ride him to the finish line, but she was going to make good on her word.

"Babe." The word came out as a warning, which she didn't heed. She stared into his eyes with a half-smile on her face.

But she couldn't stay smug for long—he pinched her nipples, twisting them with a light touch that had her grinding on him again.

"That's it. Take that cock." He bucked his hips upward, and she couldn't stay still if she tried. All willpower gone, she was helpless to his rough fingers working over her nipples and the deep throb of his cock stretching her.

Tossing her head back on a cry, she let go as the first rush of pleasure washed over her. Juices soaked his shaft, and he stiffened. When the warm spray of his cum hit her body, she lost her mind for long minutes, sucking every last moan of pleasure off his tongue in their kiss.

* * * * *

Linc slipped his bulletproof vest over his head and dropped it into place. Next to him, Lennon did the same. Then his twin turned to Linc.

"What's the deal with the ATF agent?" Lennon asked.

Linc didn't look at him, just fastened the vest around his torso. "What do you mean?"

"I mean are you takin' her home to momma?"

Giving him the barest of glances, he just grunted in response.

"You won't take her home to meet the woman who raised us singlehandedly, but you'll take her into danger to stop another shipment of guns from reaching the border."

A low noise broke from Linc as he spun to jab a finger into his brother's chest. "Not my call, man."

"I'm just sayin'—life's short. And Momma has been bugging us for grandbabies for how long now?"

Linc's gaze drilled into the pair of eyes so similar to his own. "You and I might have shared a womb, but we don't share ideas about women." He was in a shit mood and had been for days since learning Nealy was coming with Ranger Ops.

He had his own reasons for wanting to see the bastards of Operation X buried six feet under, but now that feeling was doubled. Maybe even tripled. If he could end this without bringing the woman he loved into the equation, he'd fucking do it in a heartbeat.

"Where is she?" Lennon asked.

Slicing a look at his brother, he muttered, "Waiting for us." While the thought of seeing his girl decked out in military garb kind of turned him on, he'd like it better if it was confined to the bedroom.

Lennon closed his locker and gripped Linc by the shoulder. "I've seen her in action. She can handle herself."

Linc didn't want to tell him that was what he was afraid of. When Nealy set her mind on something, she went after it.

The time it took to cross the border and set up to wait for the trucks to cross had Linc grinding his teeth. With Nealy so close, it was hard to keep from turning to her and grabbing her. It was also impossible to keep from grinding his teeth each time his buddies would joke with her.

Sully approached, and Linc looked up, shifting his weight and trying not to reveal how damn tense he was.

"You good to go, Linc?" Sully asked.

He gave a hard nod.

"We've gotta get these fuckers this time and capture them alive. We need them all squealing like pigs so we get the location of the rest of them."

"Yeah, picking up five here and there isn't cutting it. Not when they're growing in numbers like a colony of rabbits." Linc didn't mean to send a look Nealy's way, but he'd been automatically checking on her for an hour.

His captain followed Linc's gaze.

"She's part of the reason we need to end this today, man," Sully said. "It's not usual for ops teams to be working so closely with other agencies. Too much shit can go wrong."

Linc eyed him. "You think there's something up with that?" He'd been feeling it for a while now. Why was Nealy being thrown into danger this way? Not that she didn't do it on a daily—*fucking Manilo*, he reminded himself—but he'd have to say her director was coming down hard on her, giving her one of the biggest illegal weapons groups in the US to deal with.

Sully gave him a direct look that told Linc his radar wasn't off. Which only raised his hackles.

"Who do you think she pissed off in the agency?" Sully asked.

Linc shook his head. "No fucking clue, but it wouldn't surprise me if she has a lot of enemies, knowing the way she comes off at first. When we put this thing to bed, I'm going to DC and find out who's gunning for her."

Sully nodded and moved off, back to his position.

Casting another glance Nealy's direction, Linc's mind worked over the situation.

Government agencies worked together all the time, especially on big threats to state and country. But Nealy should be sidelined or behind the scenes, feeding them intel, not in the trenches with them.

Or in this case, the desert. The ride had been long and Linc had ground his teeth most of the way, so eager to pick Nealy up and plunk her in his lap, to feel the soft globes of her ass cradling his hard cock.

He pushed off the thoughts and looked around him. There was a smell in the air in these parts that made him think of bonfires and ridin' dirt bikes. Which led him to thoughts of actually doing what his twin had suggested and introducing Nealy to his mother.

When this was all over, maybe he'd take a few days off and go home, see that pony his momma was so thrilled about. And see how a city girl like Nealy fared in the country. After all, Linc wouldn't be in the Ranger Ops forever. Eventually, he'd kick back and find a nice spread of dirt to call his own. Maybe have a few horses and a yard big enough for kids and dogs to run in.

He caught Nealy staring at him. When they made eye contact, she dipped her head in hello.

Dammit, she shouldn't be out here.

Pushing out a sigh, he raised a hand to her.

She waved back, and in that moment, he felt a connection even from twenty yards away. No matter how far she got from him, she was still holding onto his heartstrings. He hoped to hell he'd made it clear to her that he felt this way. Not getting any sweet words in return was weighing on him, though. Did she feel differently or was she just not ready to say the words?

He sighed and got into position. What felt like hours passed. He glanced at his watch more than a half dozen times. When Jess, who was on his three, let out the tenth sigh, Linc spoke into the comms unit.

"I'm gettin' the feeling we've got the wrong time, place or both."

"Copy that," came Sully's response. "I'm making a call to Downs."

A minute later, Sully stood. "Party's over, folks. Move out."

Linc stood from his crouched position and let the guys pass as he waited for Nealy. Her lips were pressed into a stark line, and she looked ready to do some severe damage with that weapon she gripped.

"What's going on?" she asked.

"It happens."

"Someone tipped them off," she spat.

He let his stare drop to hers. "Could be right."

"Dammit."

"Calm down. This shit happens. We just need to regroup, get another set of orders."

"The great Lincoln Reed needs to plan ahead? What happened to barrel in and make shit up as you go?" She stopped walking to gape at him.

"That's not what I said. C'mon." He led the way to their vehicle and watched as she stowed her weapon with the rest of the guys. Before she got into the vehicle, he dragged her off some distance to keep the team from overhearing.

"If this is some attempt to keep me from —"

He cut her off with a fingertip on her lips. "I'm not keeping you from anything, babe. I was about to ask you how the hell you're not the director by now. You shouldn't be out here risking your neck. How many years do you have in?"

"Enough," she said with a low note of frustration. "A colleague with almost an identical background as mine was promoted over me."

"Why is that?"

"Probably because he has a dick."

He knew injustices still happened for women in this world, but he'd met his share of superior officers who were female.

Nealy sighed. "Maybe I wasn't ready," she said by way of finding the reasoning behind them promoting someone ahead of her. "That's why I need this. I need Operation X on my resume so I can take it back and shove it under somebody's nose and prove myself."

"And you will, when we've got the timing correct," he soothed, wanting to enfold her in his arms. But that would probably only tick her off further.

"Why are you grinning?" She settled a hand on her hip.

"Just thinkin' you'd bite the head off a rattlesnake if it meant one-upping them. I never met such a competitive woman in my life. Hell, I've hardly met a man as competitive."

"So?"

He moved in a step. "If you want to lay down some stakes, I'm willin' to take whatever dare you set."

She caught on to the soft drawl of his words and the meaning behind them. Taking one step forward, she held his stare. "Wonder who will come out on top this time?"

144

He dropped her a wink and jerked his head toward the vehicle. "Let's go home and find out."

* * * * *

Nealy watched Linc bypass the sidewalk leading to his front door.

"Where are you going?" she called out.

He tossed her a crooked grin over his shoulder. "C'mon."

She followed him around the building, past a row of dark hedges. When she spotted the flickering glow of moonlight on water, she stopped.

He came to a standstill as well, inches away. "Dare you."

"To what? Swim?"

Nodding once, he let his gaze drop to her breasts and back up to her face, leaving behind a trail of heat so scorching that she felt it to the marrow of her bones.

"How many of these apartments overlook the pool?"

"You chicken?"

"No. Just don't want to upset some family."

"Nobody will see. I'll show you mine if you show me yours."

With a swipe of her tongue over her lips, she let her gaze wander over his muscled chest, the dips and swells standing out in his dark T-shirt. Mind made up, she reached for the hem of her top. Tugging it free from her waistband, she drew it up and over her head.

The warm Texas air kissed her bare skin, and her nipples puckered inside her sports bra. Linc's steady gaze never swayed from her as he drew off his own shirt. The blue light of shadows spread over his beautiful body, carving him into that statue of David again.

Passion swept her up, and the words were suddenly there on her lips—*I love you*. But she couldn't utter them, not yet. This could all be a heat-of-the-moment affair. They were thrown together, working closely. Could she trust her emotions?

After removing his boots, he pushed his cargo pants and boxers down his hips. As his cock bounced free—hard, thick, long—she hurried to strip off her own pants. She was already damp with arousal, her nipples tightened into hard puckers. Pinching them, she stepped toward him and out of her clothing.

Bare naked, each of them, standing inches apart.

He didn't reach for her, just turned and dived into the pool. She watched his dark form cut through the water for a moment before jumping in after him. The water was warmed by the heat of the day, but it was still cool enough to refresh.

Pushing just beneath the surface, she opened her eyes underwater to make out Linc's location and saw him pop up a few feet away.

She did the same, treading water and shaking it out of her eyes. They shared a grin.

She took off again, swimming laps using various strokes, and he matched her every move, even when she dog-paddled. She giggled at the huge muscled man dog paddling and bobbed over to the edge to grip the cement.

He disappeared under the surface, and she watched him somersault before coming up next to her. Dipping her mouth under, she gathered some water, so when he came near, she spouted it at him.

The stream hit him in the cheek, and he splashed her. A squeal threatened to leave her, but she was trying to keep it down so they didn't attract any attention from the other apartment dwellers. Getting out of the pool naked with spectators around was not a happy ending to the night, in her opinion.

Swimming away, she got only a few feet before he darted in front of her.

"My brother and I used to play sharks in the community pool. Sometimes Mom put us in a summer camp while she worked days."

"Who won the shark game?" she asked.

"Usually Lennon did." He chuckled.

Nealy studied his handsome face. "You love your brother very much. Does it bother you to have him with you... on the team, I mean?"

He arched a brow. "No, why?"

"Knowing he could get hurt."

Linc's expression changed, and he twitched his head toward a few lounge chairs set up on one end of the pool. "Let's sit a while."

They swam to the steps and he strutted bare-ass to a unit with stacks of white towels. He grabbed two and tossed one at her, which she unfurled and wrapped around herself, aware of her nudity.

Her skin pebbled against the terrycloth, and she drew it closer, watching Linc bind his own towel around his hips. He sank to a lounger and opened his arms to her.

She fell into them, enveloped by warm steel and cool droplets of water. Somehow, their swim had brought her closer to him. Why or how, she wasn't sure. But seeing him in a totally different environment, doing an activity that wasn't everyday, had her looking at him closer.

There were depths to this man that she'd never guessed at back in the hospital those first days she'd known him. Then, she'd known he was tough, rugged, and stood up for what he believed in. He had a hell of a tolerance for pain and a stiff upper lip about everything he endured.

Only... he'd made it clear how much he enjoyed her presence.

Now she was cuddled against his chest, with his arms wrapped snugly around her.

And she couldn't think of any place in the world she'd rather be.

He tucked her head beneath his chin and kissed the top of her wet head. "You're not cold, are you?"

"Not at all. It's a warm night."

"Are you over your anger at what happened tonight? That we hit a dead end?"

She sighed. "It's frustrating, chasing tails sometimes. It's not as if I haven't experienced it before, but I can't say I'm very patient when I do."

He rumbled a laugh, chest vibrating against her side. "I'm quite acquainted with your patience level."

"I was just doing my job."

He flexed his arms, bringing her closer to his hard chest, her ass seated firmly over the thin terrycloth barrier between them. One slip of the towel and he'd be buried inside her.

While the sexual awareness took over her body, she had a bloom of warmth over her emotions. Being so close to Linc was something she'd never believed would happen for her. Deep down, she wasn't a woman who dwelled over who she'd marry, dreamed of her wedding dress or picked out names for her future kids ahead of time. She loved her work and her life was full.

Somehow, the universe had thrown her a curveball, though, and she'd fallen straight into the black hole of loving a wonderful man.

"Tell me more about this director of yours."

His question jarred her. Her mind was so far away from DC and Mark Mitchum. Linc must be

149

thinking on the promotion they'd spoken about earlier.

"Well, he's the acting deputy director."

"Ah."

"He took the position not long ago. And I was given this. I eagerly took the challenge, because I want to prove myself. Maybe next time an opening comes around, I'll have enough in my file to back me."

Linc asked her a few more questions about what she'd figured to be a touchy subject. But she found talking to him about it somehow knocked the situation down a peg or two on the importance scale. Like telling someone a tidbit of your life that was behind you now.

Her focus was on the present. And presently, she was in Linc's arms.

She pressed a kiss to his stubbled jaw... and around to his neck. When she lifted her head again, he kissed her, a soft brushing of lips that quickly turned to a hunger neither could—or wanted to—control.

When he broke the kiss, she climbed off his lap, and he stood from the lounger. Together, they gathered their clothing into bundles in their arms and made it back to the apartment, leaving behind the pool glimmering in the moonlight, looking as untouched as before they swam. But Nealy felt the ripples of their time together deep under the surface of her being.

Chapter Nine

Nealy lay spread eagle on Linc's bed, her firm thighs straining with the tension of holding her legs apart while he looked at every inch of her.

His cock jutted out, the tip angry and purple, but he wasn't ready to give in and bury himself in those juicy wet folds of hers. Watching her squirm was too good to miss out on.

She twisted the sheets at her sides and bit into her lower lip. "Don't torture me, Linc. I need you."

Her throaty rasp sank deep into him. It fucked with his control, his mind and every part of his body as he held back from pleasuring the one woman on earth he wanted more than the next breath of air he took.

As he looked on, she raised her fingers to her hard nipples and strummed the tips. They both moaned in reaction.

"Spread your pussy open for me. Let me see how wet you are, babe." His gritty tone reflected the inferno going on in his body. Not even his raging hard-on gave it away as much as his voice did.

Holding his gaze, she skimmed her hands down her torso to her mound. Then slipped her fingers over her outer lips, swollen and damp with juices, to part them. The instant her pink folds were exposed, a trickle of arousal ran from the tip of his cock.

"You want me," she rasped.

Fisting his cock at the base, he gave it one slow pump, squeezing more precum from the head. She wet her lips.

"You wanna suck my cock, babe? You want me in the back of your throat?"

She made a tiny noise that had him standing at the bedside, his shaft at her lips. She parted them and snaked out her tongue, and he rested his cock head on it. When she closed her lips over him, a shudder rose up from his toes. For a long minute, he allowed her to suck on his cock, drawing him into the back of her throat with deep, sucking pulls while he swayed his hips.

Feeling that familiar tingle of ecstasy closing around his nerve endings, he drew his shaft free of her mouth and stood over her, staring through hooded eyelids.

"Turn over."

His command had her eyes opening wide, but she did as he instructed, rolling into the sheets and presenting her rounded ass.

"Get on your hands and knees."

Christ, he was aching hard and dying to plunge deep inside her.

He walked around the bed and stood looking over her dipped back, her rounded globes and the wet, pink slit between her thighs.

It was too much. He couldn't hold back any longer.

Dropping to his knees, he palmed her ass, spreading her open to him. He eased in, inhaling her arousal. When he flicked the tip of his tongue over her soaking pussy, she cried out, fisted the sheets and pushed backward all in one motion.

His tongue was driven into her slit, and he moaned at the exquisite flavors coating his tongue. Need burst through him, and he rubbed his cock on the edge of the mattress just to ease a bit of the ache.

Licking her pussy up and down, curling his tongue around the hard pearl of her clit and back up to tongue-fuck her, he couldn't stop the rumble of pleasure he got from eating her out.

The clench of her pussy around his tongue told him she was about to tip over the edge, and he thumbed apart her ass again. When the cooler air hit her pucker, her body tightened. Dragging his thumb over the tiny ridges of her anus, he felt her buck in his grasp.

Holding her firmly, he continued to suck and nibble her pussy while stroking the pad of his thumb over her ass. The moment he felt her give a shudder, he knew she was lost to sensation, too far gone to even cry out.

He drove her on, taking what he wanted from her, until she sucked in sharply and let go.

Her body pulsated from head to toe. Juices flowed onto his tongue, and he lapped faster, extending her orgasm even as her pucker clamped down beneath his thumb.

When he drew away, she finally made a noise— one of regret.

His lips tipped upward. "You like that, babe."

She twisted her face in the sheets, showing him one flushed cheek, her bitten lips and her eye, glassy with pleasure.

She was far gone, and damn if it didn't turn him on even more.

Moving to his feet, he knelt on the mattress and gripped her by the hips. The head of his cock angled straight for the sweet center of her. Without willing his body to move, it did. Heat enveloped the tip of his erection, and he was burrowing into her one inch at a time until his balls were snug against her clit.

A rock of his hips brought out the moan he'd been hoping for. Then another. Soon, her cries were filling the room, and he grunted in time to them. Yanking her ass up, he edged a bit deeper.

She reared her head back, and he wrapped a fist around her hair, pulling her up for a kiss. From behind he couldn't kiss her as thoroughly as he wanted, but it was too late to change position.

He was right there, on the edge of explosion, and she was already tensing around his cock.

Blinding need took over, and he released his hold on her hair to hook his hand under her breasts, and as he pounded into her with a frantic need, he flicked her nipples.

She came apart first, and he swore to God he felt her clit pulsating against his balls. The sensation threw him overboard, and he lost all sense of anything but loving this woman.

After long seconds of spurting his cum into her body, he realized his lips were at her ear, and he was whispering "I love you" over and over again.

* * * * *

Tears of emotion tasted salty on Nealy's tongue. She collapsed onto the sheets, with her lover's cock still buried to the hilt in her and their combined release running freely out of her pussy.

Her limbs felt heavy, sated. And she couldn't move if she tried.

Linc flattened himself over her, his weight pressing her down a moment before he pulled free and rolled off. He gathered her into his arms and pressed soft kisses over her face and hair. Finally, he took her lips.

The tender kiss was full of passion, love and so much more she couldn't begin to find names for. All she knew was what lived in her heart.

Placing her palm along his chiseled jaw, she looked into his eyes. "I'm in love with you too," she whispered.

His eyes burned and took on a look of incredulousness, as if he couldn't believe she would ever say the words or feel the same about him.

A breath left him, and he pressed his forehead against hers, eyes shuttering as he ingested what she'd said.

"Christ, I don't know how. I was horrible to you from the start."

"Not always."

He opened his eye and pierced her in his very serious stare. "It was my cock, wasn't it? It's too good not to fall for."

The unexpected joke in his words set off her giggles. Then he was chuckling too, and they shook for a moment with mirth.

"I think it was more your angry glares that did it, Linc."

"How 'bout your sharp tongue? You were always slamming me for one thing or another. And those interrogation sessions…" He grunted.

She pressed her palms into his chest to lever herself up and looked into his eyes. "We had a rough start, I'll agree."

"And a slippery end." He reached between her thighs and dragged a fingertip through her soaking folds. The sensation pulled her hips off the bed, and she lost herself to the way he watched her as he fingered her again.

Gliding his digits in, out and around her clit. She never expected yet another orgasm, but soon she was coming apart for him, shaking and holding onto him.

He kissed her mouth, open on a gasp of bliss, and she tumbled into loving this man full force. No holding anything back. No barriers between them.

Now she only had to figure out how to make life with a member of the Ranger Ops team work. With separations, challenges in finding time for each other and many other things she couldn't even think of right now, it wouldn't be easy.

She wasn't about to give up her job, not when a promotion could be in her future. And he'd never ask her to leave the ATF anyway.

His light, fluttery touch on her spine had her melting into a boneless state on the edge of sleep.

"Babe."

"Hmm?" she responded.

"Come home with me and meet my momma."

She went still. She'd never been a meet-the-momma type of girl. Her relationships had been more of the quick fling that ended just as fast.

"I'd like you to meet the woman who raised me and Lennon without any help. And I want her to know the woman who finally captured me."

Her smile spread over his shoulder muscle, and she turned her lips into his warm, steely skin. "When would we go?"

"Right away. Now."

She pushed up. "Now?"

"In this line of work, I never know when I'll be called out. Can you sleep in the car on the drive there? We'd make it in time for breakfast, and my momma always makes the best breakfasts."

The spur of the moment decision to go wasn't something Nealy was accustomed to making, but what did she have to lose? A few hours of sleep. But she'd gain so much more in doing this for Linc.

Throwing herself out of bed, she smacked him in the thigh. "Let's go. Time's a-wastin'."

The grin he tossed her way warmed every corner of her body, and she wondered what she'd ever done without the man.

Especially when he donned that cowboy hat and gave her the wickedest grin imaginable.

* * * * *

Linc drew a deep breath in and held it, savoring the feel of country air in his lungs. He looked toward the house where he'd grown up. A simple white ranch without any traits to make it stand out on the

159

pages of a décor magazine, other than the big red pots of flowers flanking the door. But it was a quiet, homey place that raised a nostalgia in him to find his bag of army guys and lay out a war on the front porch with Lennon opposite him, spitting with the shooting noises he made.

Nealy got out of the car and came to stand beside him. When she took his hand, he raised it to his lips and kissed her knuckles. "I miss this place every day."

"I can see why." Her stare went to the fields on every side of the house, the small plot surrounded by farmland. The fence corralling the neighbor's horses touched the edge of his momma's yard.

"Come on. She'll have the coffee on."

"But not enough for three people," Nealy responded.

He grinned down at her. "You don't know my momma."

They stepped up to the front door, and Linc knocked. While they waited to surprise his mother with their appearance, he glanced down at the frame of the door and some notches cut into it.

He pointed. "See those? Linc caught hell for taking his pocketknife to the wood. Said he was measuring his action figures the same way we had a growth chart on the closet door."

She laughed. "Your mother must not mind much if she left the marks there."

He shook his head. Sentimental was the best word to describe his mother.

Suddenly, the door flew open and a woman hurled herself at Linc. He released Nealy's hand to catch his mother, and she bounced up and down and squealed.

"My boy! I haven't set eyes on you for so long. You must have known I was longing to see one of my boys. Or did you bring that rotten twin of yours with you?" She looked up to see Nealy standing there and pulled away.

Linc planted a kiss on his mother's cheek, but she barely registered it as she stared at Nealy.

"I'm Sheila, Linc's momma."

"Hello. I'm Nealy." She held out her hand, and his mother gave it a warm squeeze.

"Come in, come in! You'll be wanting breakfast and plenty of hot coffee, I'm guessin', if you showed up at this hour." His mother bustled to the kitchen, and they followed. Linc threw a smile at Nealy, who seemed amused and maybe a bit shell-shocked at his mother's whirlwind greeting.

"Now tell me, where did you find this beautiful woman, son?" She pulled down two more mugs and poured the coffee. "Do you take milk, dear?" she asked Nealy.

She nodded, and his mother went to the fridge. While she was there, she pulled out eggs and a pound of bacon. Linc winked at Nealy before rolling up the sleeves of his denim shirt and sidling up to the stove.

"Oh, look who's cookin' us breakfast," his momma said with a beam of pride in her eyes. She handed Nealy her coffee and passed her the milk. "Come, have a seat at the table and we'll watch this big special ops man cook us breakfast." A look claimed his mother's features. "Wait—was I supposed to keep the special ops part a secret or does Nealy know?"

"She knows. If she didn't, it's too late now." Linc chuckled as he took out a cast iron skillet and added the bacon strips. He smiled at his mom. "It's good to see you."

"You too. Oh, what a happy surprise this is. And to think I was considering going into town to the farmer's market today. I'm glad I didn't go or I might have missed you. So tell me, Nealy, how did you meet Lincoln?"

He smiled at the use of his full name, as only a momma could say it. While the bacon fried, he listened to the two most important women in his life discuss how they'd come to meet.

Nealy eyed him with a sparkle in her eyes. "We got locked in an elevator together, and that's when things really took off between us."

"Oh heavens, just like the soaps! Locked in an elevator! For how long?"

"Long enough to make me fall for her," Linc added.

His mother's cheeks flushed with pleasure, and she talked to Nealy for long minutes while Linc finished with the bacon, laying it on a plate covered with paper toweling and started on frying the eggs.

When he set two plates before his ladies, he earned big smiles in return. His heart couldn't be fuller, nor his stomach as he settled in with half a dozen eggs for himself, bacon and a pile of toast and jam on the side.

Nealy watched him tuck in, shaking her head. "I've never seen a man eat like that."

"You don't know my boys. I had to work two jobs just to keep them fed! The milk we used to go through..." She shook her head, and Nealy laughed.

"We thought we'd walk out and see the neighbor's new foal," Linc said.

"He's grown a foot this week, I swear," his momma said, pushing aside her empty plate. "How long will you be staying?" She looked between them.

"Just for the day. We've gotta get back to the city."

"Well, you must enjoy every minute you have out of that rat-race. See the horses, sit a spell on the deck and we'll have some iced tea I just whipped up this morning."

"I can't imagine anything more lovely," Nealy said with an earnest tone. Linc studied the fresh bloom in her cheeks and her easy smile. It seemed they both had needed some time away from reality to unwind.

He took care of the dishes, rinsing them and putting them into the dishwasher. Then he held out his hands, one for each of this ladies, and helped them to their feet. They went outside to see the horses and enjoy the rest of the morning together.

Chapter Ten

Nealy had never seen Linc so at ease. His legs kicked out, reclining in a lounge chair, and his eyes half-lidded against the sun in the distance. The shade offered enough cool to keep them happy, as did the ice-cold glasses of tea on a low table between them.

His momma had sipped hers for a minute with them before getting a phone call from one of her friends. While she was inside, Nealy and Linc just sat in silence.

She took his hand and squeezed it. He turned his attention to her, lips quirked at the corner. "You've been wonderful today, babe," he said.

"So have you. I've seen a different side to you."

He cocked a brow. "I hope that's a good thing."

She nodded. "I think so."

"I see a difference in you too." He released her fingers to lift a hand to her cheek. "You're more beautiful in the country air."

She laughed. "I'm not sure how to take that, since I'm not in the country very often."

A crinkle appeared between his brows. "What do you think about the country?"

"I love it. I admit I haven't had many experiences with rural living or vacations even."

"But what would you say about retiring someplace like this someday?"

She met his eyes. They burned with the intensity of his question she knew was much more than he was saying to her. She couldn't speak for a minute.

"With me," he added quietly.

"Linc…"

He cradled her face, and she leaned into his hand. "I don't expect you to make a decision right now, but just sayin'… someday, I want this. And I want you with me."

A gasp of a breath from behind them had both her and Linc turning to look at his mother standing feet away, her hand over her mouth and eyes wide.

"Did you just ask her to marry you?"

Nealy flushed hot, and she knew her face was scorching. "Oh no, he didn't propose. We were just talking nonsense."

Linc sat up.

Drifted to one knee on the deck.

And took her by the hands.

Nealy gaped at him. Surely not. He wouldn't be proposing to her on the fly like this, in front of his momma, only what… months after their first meeting? They'd only just decided they even liked each other. Up until recently, they'd been at each other's throats every minute they could be.

Her heart thudded harder and harder. Linc held her gaze prisoner, and he seemed completely chill as he said, "Nealy, I want you to know how I feel about you. I love you more than I ever believed possible. And I want to spend my life with you. It won't be easy. We'll have struggles and worries, especially given our careers. But I want to do it all with you. And with my momma as witness, I'm asking you to be my wife. I promise to be there for you every step you take and love you with every fiber of my being for the rest of my days."

The lump in Nealy's throat cut off any words that she tried to emit. A tear seeped from the corner of her eye and rolled down her cheek. "Linc. Oh God, Linc. Yes, I'll marry you!" She hurled herself at him, knocking him back on the lounge chair that creaked under their weight.

His lips found hers, and she succumbed to all the emotions flowing through her as she kissed her fiancé for the first time, thinking of how many more kisses and how many more firsts there would be for the two of them.

Today was the beginning of the rest of their life, and she'd never forget it as long as she lived.

When they broke away, his momma gave a loud sniff. Laughing, they broke apart to look at the woman, who was as happy for her son as a momma could ever hope to be.

"I've never imagined having a daughter, but if I had, she'd be just like you, Nealy." She came forward to hug them both.

* * * * *

Linc watched Nealy roll her garments and stow them into her carryon bag efficiently. Her hair swung down, partially covering her face, and he had a feeling there was a reason why she hadn't brushed it away yet.

He sank to the mattress next to the bag, but she didn't glance his way.

When she moved to stuff a pair of panties into the bag, he snatched them out of her hand and brought them to his nose.

Her jaw dropped—at least he'd gotten a reaction from her.

Drawing in a deep breath of her panties perfumed with her personal scent, he looked at her over the lace. When her gaze met his, he saw the worry there in the depths as plain as it was to look at a blue sky and then see the sun.

He dropped the panties. "You're worried."

She bit her lower lip, and he tried not to think of towing her down onto the mattress with him and settling her over his cock. There would be plenty of time for that later.

"Nealy." He took her hand and squeezed it. "Tell me what's bugging you."

168

"It's going back to DC," she said. "With no resolution, nothing solid to hand to my superiors and say I've made progress. Why should they put their faith in me if I haven't gotten them anything to bite into? Since I've taken over the case, I've had few arrests, a few hundred guns recovered. Nothing like the number still out there."

"You're only as good as those backing you. If they're not providing the details you need to nab these assholes, how can you be solely responsible for that?"

She hesitated and finally shook her head. "I can't lean on excuses for my failures."

He hated seeing the pressure she put on herself, but what could he say to her when he did the same to himself?

Catching her other hand in his grasp, he drew her closer to stand between his knees. "I know what you're going through. Do you know how pissed off I am that I haven't put every last motherfucker from Operation X in cuffs and stuffed in the back of a police van for what they did to me?" He released her hand and rubbed at his thigh, the skin still reddened and crinkled from the burns he'd suffered.

Her stare locked on his. "Do you think I don't want justice for what they did to you as well? This isn't only about my job and a possible promotion down the road, Linc."

His heart flooded with love for her. Unable to resist, he pulled her down across his knees, holding her close. "You're an amazing woman, but you don't need to fight my battles for me."

"And you don't need to reason away mine by saying I'm not getting enough backing from the ATF."

He had to say it. "But why are you working alone on this?"

She blinked at him. "Because the chief of staff saw something in me and gave me an opportunity."

"Is it usual for an agent to work solo on a case as big as this?"

She considered the question in silence for a moment. "Because I'm working with Ranger Ops, they're probably counting on enough backup and support."

He nodded. He'd seen that sort of thing with everything from bomb squads to harbor patrols. Once they called in the special forces, they didn't need their own service to assist.

He still couldn't shake some scratchy feeling at the back of his brain about Nealy's case, though. Maybe he was just being paranoid. Nobody was out to crush her—it was just another agency's way of doing business, bullshit as it seemed to him.

When she tipped to her feet and resumed packing, he sat there watching and not saying anything. She seemed so lost in her thoughts that he didn't want to interrupt in case she was having a stroke of genius.

After she zipped the bag and lifted the handle, he stood and took it from her.

"Thanks, hon," she said with a ghost of a smile.

He cupped her chin and leaned in to brush his lips across hers. "You're going back to DC to have a meeting, talk through new intel and get new insights. Then you'll be coming right back here. And we will finish it."

At the hard, gritty tone in his voice, a trace of a smile blew across her beautiful features. But it was gone too soon, and she was solemn again as they locked up the apartment and got into his car.

On the drive to the airport, she picked at a fingernail so ruthlessly, he thought she might pull it completely off. Reaching across the seats, he covered her hand with his. She looked up at him.

"What happens to us, Linc? After we finish this, I mean? I can't be back in DC while you're here with the team."

He'd thought about it a lot—all night, in fact. How her dreams of a promotion would keep her in DC and he'd have some tough decisions to make concerning his own life.

He fucking loved the Ranger Ops, and the idea of abandoning them or some other asshole taking his spot made him want to grind up a bag of nails between his teeth. He hadn't shared a bit of his thinking with Nealy, though, knowing she would tune into his distress over it all. He wasn't going to put her in a position where she would have to choose between something she loved and him. Ever.

The flight left in an hour, and she had just enough time to get to the airport and check in. So when they slowed, and then crawled to a halt behind a long line of traffic, he felt the crunch of getting her there on time.

She bounced her knee and took out her phone. "What's going on?" she asked, flipping open an app to look at the road reports.

Craning his neck, he said, "I think it's an accident."

"Dammit. How long do you think it will take? How late do you think I can check in? Getting through security takes ages, even carrying a badge."

He nodded and sat there a minute, considering his options. He was far from the next street to exit the highway, but there might be a way to do a U-turn, if he skipped across the median, and backtracked a few streets to take another route. He just couldn't get out to make a turn until the line of traffic moved a bit.

And that wasn't happening anytime soon.

Minutes ticked by.

Nealy dropped her phone into her lap. "Crap!"

"I'll figure something out."

She stared at him, obviously losing her cool the longer they sat there. "I can't miss this meeting. It makes me look incompetent and not at all ready to take over a director position."

"Nealy, you're stuck in an accident, unable to move. Someone's going to understand —"

"You don't know how competitive these positions are, Linc. Add in how damn difficult it is for a woman still in this day and age to move up…" She shook her head, cutting off her words.

Tightening his lips, he said, "What do you want me to do? I'll abandon the car right here, right the fuck now and carry you on my shoulders all the way if that's what you want."

They were back to arguing but now that they were engaged, locked into this for the long haul, it just felt like negotiation.

Or foreplay.

He was getting hard.

"Stop looking at me like that!"

"Like what?"

"Like you want to get into the back seat and —"

"Lick your pussy till everyone in this traffic jam hears you scream? I fucking do."

"Oh my God, Linc…" She wasn't unaffected either. Her nipple hardened to a gumdrop beneath her plain white blouse that was her usual uniform attire.

"Babe, I'm here to please. If you want me to toss you in the back and rip off your clothes, that's what I'll do."

She looked at him, and he gave her a grin. Ducking her head, she bit back her own smile. "I want that too, but I'll never forgive myself if I miss this flight. If you could find a Marine buddy with a helicopter to drop a cable and lift me out of this mess and take me to the airport, that'd be good."

His mind stuttered to a stop. He took out his phone and punched in a contact.

She stared at him. "Tell me you're joking."

"I can't get a chopper, but I might be able to get something just as good."

A minute later, the first flashing lights came up from behind the line of traffic, forcing every car off to the side in order to clear enough roadway to drive.

"Holy shit, Linc. I wasn't serious about you pulling some hero strings!" Nealy twisted in excitement to look out the back window.

When the flashing lights of a Texas Rangers patrol car passed, Linc pulled out. Another patrol car slipped in behind him, escorting them to the head of the traffic jam, where a firetruck and some medic units were attending to the crash victims.

Once they were out of the line and able to hit the junction for the airport, Nealy let out a scream of victory and pumped her fist into the air. She reached over the seat, grabbed his head and yanked him in for a kiss.

With one eye on the road and his tongue in her mouth, he hadn't felt happier all day.

She plunked back into her seat. "There's nothing you wouldn't do for me, is there, Linc?"

He sent her a long look. "Now you've got the idea. You're my woman now, and I'll move fucking hills and mountains for you, babe."

* * * * *

Nealy rested her head against the back of the cab seat and tried to adjust to touching down in DC. It wasn't far from Texas to Washington, but she felt jet-lagged. Maybe it was the change of scenery. The loss of the big Texas sky she'd gazed at with such tranquility back at Linc's momma's house.

They'd found the horse and its new foal, and they were tamed enough to let her and Linc get closer. Though the mother wouldn't allow them to touch her baby, Nealy had been thrilled by the foal's long eyelashes and gangly legs, and the way it trotted with so much wild abandon had her wishing for more out of life.

Was this city, with its constant political blanket cloaking the people, the concrete jungle and government offices what she wanted forever? If she got a promotion, she'd be locked in. Trapped in the ATF office and out of the field.

As the cab crept through the heavy traffic, she couldn't help but think she might have escaped the executioner's blade when the promotion was given to Mark Mitchum.

175

"Can we go any faster?" she asked the cabbie.

He threw her an amused look. "You know anything about this city at all, lady?"

She sighed and avoided glancing at her watch. "Yes, I do."

She knew it wasn't a small town in Texas and she didn't have Linc at her side.

Shaking her head, she thought of him calling in a Texas Rangers escort through the traffic in order to get her to the airport in time.

She still couldn't believe it.

The fact she was engaged to a man like that was even more stunning.

Or the idea that he'd actually proposed in front of his momma. It spoke of how close he was to the woman, and how he wanted to bring Nealy into that world he loved.

In that moment when he'd slipped onto one knee and taken Nealy's hand in his, he'd inducted her into his life and she still felt the effects warming her heart.

A horn blast raised her from her thoughts, reminding her she was far from Texas.

There were ATF offices in about a dozen locations in the Lonestar state. Would she be happy with a sideways move?

To be with Linc, she might be.

The only other option for keeping a relationship going between them was for him to leave Ranger Ops.

How could she ask such a thing of a man who'd built a homemade bomb, knowing he would be blowing himself up, just to get back to them?

Each of them would have to make some sacrifice or another. But she didn't really see making a transition to one of the Texas offices as ditching her dreams. Just making a step in another direction, which in time might lead to other opportunities.

She had some time to make up her mind, but the decision felt halfway made, if she was honest with herself.

With that concern set aside, she had time to focus on the meeting she was about to walk into.

Mitchum's order to return had caught her off guard, but of course after their failure to make the arrest on their last mission, action must be taken.

She was either in for an ass-chewing or this was only a meeting to touch base and refresh her goals, provide new information. Why it couldn't be shared by phone or their encoded system was the big question in her mind, though.

They wanted her in person, and there must be a reason for that.

When she finally got into the ATF floor, she straightened her shoulders and strode through the office to Mitchum's door, ignoring everyone. She walked right into his office without being invited and dropped her bag to the floor.

"You called and I'm here."

177

He looked up at her, brow arched. "Hello, Agent Alexander. Glad you could make it."

She eased into a chair and crossed her legs. The only way to get through this was to dig deep and find her self-confidence. "You wanted to see me."

Tossing a look at the clock on the wall, he said, "You're late."

So he was going to be an asshole. She could handle assholes.

Smiling, she answered, "The plane had to taxi longer than expected. I'm sure you understand."

He smiled back, but there was no friendliness in it. She tried to keep her nerves off her face. He must really be ticked at her performance, and while he was her director, she couldn't help but wonder if he had other reasons for being a dick. While she'd always felt he was fake with everyone, she did wonder what was causing this extreme behavior, when typically he'd hide his true personality behind a mask of smiles and claps on the back.

She smoothed a wrinkle in her trousers. "I gather some of the information you need to share with me is too sensitive to share except in person."

"Yes." He studied her, and she kept her expression blank.

"I think you know the agency is not very happy with the outcome of the last mission. Why was the group not where we pinpointed them to be at that time?"

She arched a brow. "I was just as surprised as you are."

"You have no insights as to why they weren't there, Alexander?" He sat back and rocked slightly in his seat.

"None whatsoever. They simply never showed."

"You waited for them?"

"We waited all night. Finally, the Ranger Ops' captain called it off. The call came from Colonel Downs. The sun was rising and the new shift was coming onto border patrol. Operation X wasn't going to risk crossing with fresh personnel on the scene, ready to strip that truck down from top to bottom if necessary. Especially with alerts out for trucks carrying pig manure."

"You realize your paycheck is not signed by the Ranger Ops, correct, Nealy?"

"Well, *Mark*, I do realize I don't answer to the captain, but I trusted his judgment. Is that not why you sent me to work with them? This is a co-op, is it not?"

"It is," he said at once, reaching for his pen. He flipped it end over end. She knew it was a distraction tactic. He was trying to throw her off her game, but it wasn't going to work.

"Tell me why I'm here," she demanded.

He looked at her a moment in silence, then dropped the pen. "We've got something big on the radar."

179

"How big?"

"It's the equivalent of enemy aircraft in our airspace."

"Literal jets bringing the arms into the country or are you waxing poetic on me?"

His eyes gave off a gleam that told her he didn't like being challenged by her, but he quickly squelched it.

"It's by water. They're coming through a port city. A ship that remains just out of the harbor, avoiding patrols there. But small vessels will be waiting, and they can easily slip past as fishermen or pleasure boaters."

She glanced around at the empty seats on either side of her. "Why am I the only person being told this? I thought this was a meeting."

"It is. Between me and you. The others have already been informed. I'm telling you because you were off in Texas not fulfilling your duties."

That struck her. How many eyes did he have on her? Did the ATF know she'd been living with Linc in his apartment and even gone to the countryside to visit his mother? For all she knew, they had photos of Linc on bended knee and tears rolling down her face as she said yes to his marriage proposal.

She got mad. All that was on her personal time. She wasn't holding hands with Linc and skipping to the scenes of these crimes.

But was she being proactive enough? By waiting for information to trickle down from her office, she might be missing something she ordinarily might have seen for herself, if she had been the one on the sidelines doing the digging.

Which made her remember the last time she'd unearthed her own intel and gotten an ass-reaming for it.

"I think we both know no agent is as dedicated as I am. I got that flash drive you asked for, didn't I?"

"Yes, and the coordinates were even off," he muttered, grabbing his pen and flipping it again.

She stared at him. Her heart gave a little lurch, which she didn't know how to interpret.

The coordinates *had* been off, but how did he know? He must have gotten a report from Sully.

No matter. She had a boot to shove up Mitchum's ass, and she was damn well doing it before she left this office today.

Leaning over the desk, she looked Mitchum in the eyes. "Now we both know I have more experience in the field than you do yourself, *Acting Deputy Director Mitchum*." She emphasized his title and stood and tapped his desk with a palm. "And usually that takes a person far in this agency."

He blinked at her but said nothing.

Nealy went on, "I'll take everything you have on this port, the times arranged for rendezvous and all the details on the number of men we're facing and approximation of weapons that will be smuggled into the country. I'll catch the next flight out." She'd already checked into the flight details and knew it wasn't booked full. Also, that she could be back in Texas within the day.

Without waiting for more, she picked up her bag and left his office, sailing out and not giving a backward glance.

Her mind was made up now. She was finished with Mitchum's threatening undertones, and she wasn't going to be under his thumb for long. As soon as she locked up Operation X, she was making the shift to Texas. She wasn't only going to be a Texas wife—she was going straight to an airport shop and buying herself a nice pair of cowgirl boots.

Get ready, Texas. There's a new ATF agent in town.

* * * * *

Linc settled his ass on the barstool, aware of how long it'd been since he planted himself at a bar with his buddies. Too long.

"Man, it's good to have you back." Lennon clapped him on the back and took up the next stool. He waved at the pretty bartender with the dazzling smile he gave all women he might want in his bed later and ordered a round of whiskey for all six of them.

Shaw got his glass in hand first and lifted it. Everyone looked to him as he stared at Linc and said, "To Linc."

"To Linc," they echoed and tossed back the alcohol.

It burned a warm current straight through Linc's system, and he relaxed bit by bit. Until now, he hadn't realized how fucking edgy he was that Nealy had boarded that plane this morning.

The afternoon had been taken up with some boring ass chores like washing his sheets and then hitting the gym at the apartment complex for an hour. When Sully had called everyone together for drinks, Linc had been eager to get out.

He set his glass down on the bar top and rested his elbows there too. Next to him, Lennon asked for another. "You want one, bro?"

He shook his head. "Not yet."

"Where's your woman?"

Linc eyed him.

The bartender pushed Lennon's drink across the bar to him with a flirty wink. He grinned back and looked her up and down. When she was called off to serve another customer, Linc shook his head.

"Dude, she's gonna throw out a hip walking that way."

Lennon brought the glass to his lips. "You can't deny it's a pretty view."

Linc didn't respond. He wasn't getting sucked into discussing women with his brother when Nealy was ingrained so deep into his mind that she left behind not just furrows but canyons.

"Heard you visited Momma." Lennon gave him a side-eye.

Linc grunted. "She called you?"

"With news like that, it's a wonder she didn't organize a parade and spots on late-night talk shows. I'm pretty sure I did see a YouTube commercial heralding the news of your engagement, though."

Linc chuckled. Maybe he did need that drink, after all.

He waved the bartender over. She came with the bottle of whiskey in hand and eyed both him and Lennon as she poured two fingers' worth. "You brothers?"

"Twins. I'm the hot one. He's engaged." Lennon sent an elbow into Linc's, making him slosh some alcohol over the rim of his glass.

The bartender grabbed a white bar towel and mopped up the mess while leaning in to talk to his brother.

From beside him, Jess tipped toward him. "Did I just hear the E word, man?"

Great. He wasn't ready to tell his drinking buddies that he was the next Ranger Ops man to fall prey to saying I do. He, Lennon, Jess and Cav had formed a club of sorts, especially after losing Shaw and Sully.

"Yeah, it's true," he said to Jess.

"Wow. Man." He blew out a low whistle that drew Cav's attention from beside him.

"What are we talkin' about?" Cav asked, moving back to get a good view of Linc.

"Our boy's getting married. He's given up, and now all hope is lost. He's got to get his golf game up and buy that minivan to fit his two-point-five kids and all their soccer buddies." Jess gave a humorless laugh.

Cav winced and lifted his empty glass to alert the bartender he needed a refill. When she came over, he said, "We all need one." She went down the line, refilling glasses for all six of the Ranger Ops team. Cav raised his high. "To Linc. One of our fallen."

"Wait, what the hell's going on?" Shaw asked from down the line.

This method of rumor running from one ear to the next was getting on Linc's nerves. He set down his glass, climbed onto his barstool and looked down at the guys. "I'm getting married. Yes, it's true, guys. I'm out of the prowling game but I can still drink y'all under the table, and I plan to give it a damn good run tonight! Whiskey for everyone!"

The bar was rushed by all the customers wanting a piece of Linc's dollar bill, and he dropped back to the stool to toss back his own.

"Holy shit. I never thought you would have stopped taking every beautiful woman you could to your bed, man," Jess said, shaking his head as if terrible news had just befallen them all. "That ATF agent really got to you, didn't she? I'll say she's gorgeous and has a fucking killer body but—"

He leveled a look at his friend. "How 'bout we don't talk about her body anymore?"

"Okay. We'll talk about hers instead." He gestured to the bartender, who was swaying her hips so much that Linc was pretty sure she'd have all the bottles knocked over and broken by the end of the night.

"They fall all over us, have you noticed?" Lennon asked.

"Yeah, I have. But I don't care anymore." Linc looked at his brother. "Are you too drunk to remember if I ask you to come along with me and shop for a ring?"

Lennon set his glass down with a thump and twisted to Linc. "You're asking me?" He threw a splayed hand over his chest with a fake flutter of his lashes. "It's like we're besties or something! I can't believe it. Guys! I'm going ring shopping with Linc!"

"Dickhead." Linc hid his grin behind his glass.

The others tormented him with gushes of teasing that would have put a housewife reality show to shame. They continued to carry on for some time. Somebody ordered appetizers and about a dozen dipping sauces to go with them. Which led to steak dinners and more whiskey.

When Linc had had his fill of alcohol for one evening and a belly stuffed with steak and all the jalapeno poppers he could handle, he stood and got out his wallet.

"Wait, you're leavin'?" Lennon asked.

"Yeah, I'm headin' home."

"Pussy whipped already. Gonna stop off and shop for that minivan on your way?"

Linc gave him a grin. "Yep. I'll be pickin' your ass up in it tomorrow first thing so we can shop for that ring."

"I'd at least look up some ratings on those automatic doors that always quit working before you sign the deal." Lennon waved away the bills Linc was trying to throw down to cover his bill. "I got this."

"You sure?"

"Yeah. Not every day your twin brother asks a woman to marry him. Let me buy you a steak at least."

"Don't forget the whiskey you bought everyone in the house. I'll do the same for you when it's your time." He gripped his brother's shoulder.

Lennon looked at him as if he'd just killed his dog. "Don't ever let me hear you speak such dirty words again. Momma would wash your mouth out with soap. Now get on home and call that girl of yours. I know you've been dyin' to all night."

187

Linc squeezed Lennon's shoulder. "See you tomorrow, bro."

As Linc moved down the line of guys, they all gave him nods. His chest swelled with affection for these idiots he called friends and teammates. They were all his brothers too, and he couldn't survive without them.

But right now, he was hoping to go home and hear from his girl. His fiancée. The woman he never believed would come along and tame his wild streak. One thing Jess had said tonight stuck out to him.

She was beautiful—and she had a killer body. And Linc couldn't wait to get her alone in that pool under the moonlight again.

Chapter Eleven

"Who are we waitin' on? Colonel Downs?" Linc stared at his teammates seated around the table.

Sully kept his face neutral, but Linc noted a ripple in the tendon at the crease of his jaw at his question. Whatever it was... it had to be big. Which meant Linc was leaving without saying goodbye to Nealy. He hadn't heard from her since she texted to tell him she'd touched down in DC and was on her way to see her director.

After that, nothing. He'd sent her a few texts but got no responses, and to say he was worried was the understatement of the decade. He didn't like not knowing where she was or the reason she was in DC in the first place. For all he knew, she'd been dispatched to another city on some other mission to take down a sadistic fucking drug lord like Manilo.

Great—he was traveling down that rabbit hole again. After she'd shared that bit of information with him, Linc had dug into the history of the case, and it was fucking terrifying enough considering a lot of details weren't made available to the public.

Just thinking about Nealy neck-deep in dangers he couldn't protect her from made him grind his teeth.

Lennon turned his head to pierce him in his gaze. Realizing the noise he was making and the damage he was doing to his pearly whites, he relaxed his jaw muscles and templed his fingers on the table instead.

Minutes passed with nobody speaking.

Suddenly, the door flew open and the most beautiful woman in the world sailed in, wearing a self-confidence that had his dick standing up and saluting.

He jumped to his feet, but Nealy sent him a look that kept him rooted in place. It was clear by the expression on her face that something big was in fact going down, she knew what it was... and she would inevitably be joining them for.

He dropped into his seat again and thank God for Colonel Downs getting the team new chairs that weren't about to collapse under his weight, because he wasn't gentle about it.

Her gaze skimmed over him and landed on their captain. Stepping forward, she set her bag on the floor and took up the head of the table. All eyes focused on her.

When she began to talk, spilling details about a ship coming in with enough weapons in the hull to put a gun in the hands of every preschooler in the state of Texas, where to find this ship and how to go about stopping it, they all leaned forward to listen.

Linc's ear was tuned in as well, but so was his body and his heart. He was damn proud of his girl. If she wasn't promoted within the year, he'd be shocked. Her skills and no-failure attitude was exactly what shot a person to the top. She'd be next, he was sure of it.

"There's a truck pulling out in thirty minutes," she said. "We'll travel disguised as one of the many trucks that transport these weapons from the fishing and pleasure boats."

"I hope we won't be riding in pig shit," Linc said, garnering remorseful chuckles from his team. They all knew what he'd suffered and none of them wanted to relive that shit.

"After we arrive?" Lennon asked.

She looked to him. "We split up. Some stay with the truck. Some take a boat out to the ship."

Sully was shaking his head. "As captain, I can't see that as being a good path for any of us. We're stronger together."

"But we all know that to take down a bunker, you have to spread out and enter through both the front and back doors."

Linc was shaking his head. "Sully's right. We stick together as a team. Power in numbers."

"Guts and glory, man," Lennon said, bumping knuckles with Jess to his left.

"Gear up. We roll out in thirty minutes. We'll make a plan on the way." Sully stood and left the room, leaving Linc wondering why he hadn't stayed and fought for his team more. Maybe because he had no intention of arguing with Nealy in front of everyone and would save it for the ride to the coast.

The others got up and followed their captain, but Linc remained in place. He and Nealy's gazes met across the table.

"You okay?" he said softly.

She dropped her eyes and nodded. "I get the feeling Sully's not on board with my tactics."

"Honestly, I can see why. It's always a bad idea to go in separately unless you have several units on the scene like we had with Knight Ops."

She compressed her lips, and his stare zeroed in on them. "I should call them in."

He nodded. "Team Rou too. We need all hands on deck."

"This all has to be orders from superior officers."

"Better get on it, director." He stood, palms on the table.

She blinked. "Why did you call me that?"

"Because you're ready, even if the idiots in your agency don't see it yet. You'll be seated in a cozy office handing out orders sooner than you think." He dropped her a wink and walked out of the room. Though he wanted to touch her badly, it wasn't a good idea. They had to stay focused, and one fingertip on her smooth, freckled skin would make him lose his mind.

She didn't follow him, and as he geared up, he thought about what they were getting into. By the time they all met up and made it to their transport, the operation had tripled with Knight Ops and Team Rou on the ground en route to the coastal meeting point.

Sully caught Linc's eye. Linc stopped walking, knowing his captain wanted a word.

"You good on this, man?" Sully asked.

"'Course."

"You know if it means one person or the team, it's the team, right?"

Linc stared at him. He knew what he was asking of him, and he didn't want to fucking think about it. The concept wasn't something the Ranger Ops ever spoke of—they all knew that the mission came first, even if one of theirs fell.

If the fallen was Nealy...

He shook his head. "I got it, Sully."

His captain closed his hand over Linc's shoulder and squeezed. "She's strong and can hold her own. Remember that. She's with you and Lennon."

"Then she'll be safe."

When Sully met his gaze, something subtle passed between them. He'd do anything for his wife and understood Linc's position when it came to Nealy.

As they all climbed into the truck, he was pleased when she squeezed in next to him, her thigh touching his.

* * * * *

Ranger Ops was sandwiched between Knight Ops and Team Rou. With that sort of firepower flanking them, they had no reason to be worried at all.

Except Nealy was as jittery as a caffeine addict after several hits of espresso. She fought to keep from bouncing her knee or tapping a foot and alerting an enemy to her position.

The darkness cloaked them completely, and she couldn't even make out Linc next to her until he turned the whites of his eyes on her.

This was it — the biggest moment of her career. If they pulled this off, she would have proven herself.

Dragging in a deep breath of the salty Gulf air, she shifted the weapon in her hands in order to ease the weight. Linc was looking at her, and she could see a question in his eyes, but no one spoke.

Several more minutes passed. Finally, Shaw breathed out, "I see it. Shadow making its way to harbor at our two."

Nealy turned her head to peer into the darkness, barely making out the hulking outline of the ship's bow.

Her heart pounded harder. This was it. She had gone over the instructions so many times they were engraved on her brain. But still, she went over them one more time to ensure she wouldn't forget her role.

She was with Linc and Lennon. The three of them would take the first boat they saw, neutralize whoever was on the boat and head out to meet the weapons ship.

As it came a bit closer, the size and ominous look to the vessel had her issuing a breath.

"Jesus," Linc murmured at her side. "How the fuck this thing ever got into US waters is insane. They have to be paying someone off."

She'd been thinking the same since learning the ship was even slated to come in. But that wasn't her job to find out who the smugglers were in bed with — not today. She needed to be part of the forces that stopped them. With any luck, they'd have every last member of Operation X in handcuffs in time for breakfast.

Darting a look at the big man at her side, she stifled a feminine sigh. She hadn't even gotten a proper hello from him.

Warmth spread over her insides like a slick of honey. She ignored it, and just in time, because the word came in from Sully.

"Both Reeds and Alexander, here's your cue."

She gulped down her rising excitement, mingled with a healthy spot of fear, and rushed through the night with the men flanking her. Knowing Linc, he'd threatened Lennon within an inch of his life to stay on her six, because the man did not move a boot out of step. He kept perfect pace with her, inches from her back, and Linc was directly ahead.

In the darkness, she made out a small boat being loaded into the water and men jumping into it. One pushing off.

But Linc reached them before that happened. There was a splash and another, and suddenly two of the men were yanked overboard. Nealy did her part by clubbing a third over the head. He fell in a boneless slump in the boat, and Linc grabbed him by the shirt and dragged him out too.

Together, Linc and Lennon hauled all three to the shore, where some men from Team Rou, suddenly appearing out of the darkness like the spirit their team was named after, took it from there. She didn't have time to watch them truss the guys up like hogs or gag them and load them into the truck. Linc touched her shoulder, and she turned back for the small craft.

Getting on the water was a blur to her. Small silver-tipped waves licked up the sides of the boat, which Lennon and Linc rowed with strong pulls on the oars. She wished it was light enough to watch her fiancé's muscles.

Later. If we make it out of this alive.

We have to make it out alive. We can't let down his sweet momma. She's waiting for the wedding.

Her own parents still knew nothing about her engagement, something she wanted to remedy as soon as this was over. Maybe a long weekend in

196

Miami was in the future as well. She could envision Linc on a beach in Hawaiian-print swim trunks and her mother doting over him with cold drinks while Linc talked the latest game scores with her father.

His gaze was on her, the whites enhancing the intensity of his stare. "Destination in three," he said quietly.

She nodded and gripped her weapon, ready to take action.

"Holy shit, guys. Heads up."

The directive came from one of the captains into their comms units. She jerked her head up, and Linc was already fixated on the ship they were nearing. It didn't appear to be manned at all, moving swiftly through the water as if on autopilot. It definitely wasn't anchoring in the harbor as expected.

"Linc, get your team onto that vessel—now." That came from Sully.

Nealy's heart slammed her ribs. She gripped the side of the boat she was on. "What's happening?"

"Decoy ship maybe. For all we know, the real ship's down the coast unloading a quarter million weapons."

"Dammit! We can't let that happen."

"We're stretched out along this coast. There's no fucking way there's a second ship. But they knew we were here—somebody tipped them off. Look—there aren't enough boats on the water to even transport

197

the weapons. Looks like some got the memo and others didn't," Lennon said.

"Those others would be us," Linc bit off. With two more strong pulls on the oars, they were within reach of the ship's hull.

Lennon pulled out a rope and made a perfect throw, as planned. He tossed a grin back to his twin. "All those years of lassoin' the neighbor's cattle did some good, eh, bro?" He grabbed hold and shimmied upward.

Linc looked to her next. "I'm right behind you. If you fall in the water—"

"I won't," she said and took hold of the rope. She'd trained for this her entire career, and she wasn't about to let the teams—or herself—down.

When she slipped over the rail, Lennon was there to steady her. Linc landed beside her a second later. Then the three of them took off to find whoever was sailing this thing.

＊ ＊ ＊ ＊ ＊

Linc couldn't believe what he was seeing. There wasn't a fucking human in sight. It was as if the huge ship was a toy boat operated by remote control. It didn't add up.

When he led the way down a short galley ladder into the hull, crate upon crate rose up to greet him. Just the smell of raw wood used for the crates had his guts churning.

He breathed out hard and struggled to gain another breath.

"Linc. Man, it's all right. Nobody's going to put you in one of these." Lennon's low words had Linc recovering fast—and looking for a fight.

Finger poised on the trigger, he mentally egged the fuckers to step out and show their faces.

But further investigation turned up no one.

"What if it's a trojan horse?" Nealy whispered.

Jesus, he hadn't thought of that, hundreds of people hiding inside these crates just waiting to pop out.

He strode to a crate, and using the butt of his rifle, bashed the lid off one. A peek inside revealed only the black, inky shapes of firearms by the hundreds.

Lennon shook his head. "Holy hell, there's a lot of them."

The ship gave a sudden lurch, and Linc made a grab for Nealy. "What the hell's happening?"

"Guys, you're changing direction, headed back out into the Gulf. Get the hell off that thing," came Sully's order.

Linc's heart raced, and he stared down into the eyes of the love of his life. No, he wasn't letting even a single hair on her beautiful head be harmed.

The door slammed to the upper deck, cutting off all light and pitching the three of them into blackness.

"Someone's onboard," Lennon was saying to the team, spitting out rapid-fire instructions for their rescue.

Nealy's breathing was harsh and fast. Linc used his headlamp to shed light on her, but he wished he hadn't. He might not ever get the sight of her fear out of his mind for as long as he lived.

She put out a hand for him, and he took it, squeezing her gloved fingers hard. "We're locked in," she said

The worry in her voice didn't help the rising panic inside him. No fucking way was this happening a second time in his life.

They were moving. The lapping sound of waves at the outsides of the hull made him turn to search for a porthole.

"Find a way to get off that fucking thing—now," Sully commanded.

Linc exchanged a look with Lennon. They needed a plan of action.

Nealy's face was a blank mask. He reached for her to pull her in and dispel her fear, but then he saw her give an all over shudder that wasn't terror.

It was anger.

"It's fucking Mitchum behind it all." Her tone scorched over him like a wildfire.

His gaze shot to hers. "Your director."

"Yep. He said something about the coordinates being off when I was sent after the flash drive. And when I dug up some other things, he got agitated."

Linc's blood ran cold. "Sully?" he said in a harsh tone.

"Here, Linc."

"Did you at any time share the information on exactly where I found that flash drive with the ATF?"

"Fuck no."

"There's your answer," Lennon said, serious as a sinner in hell.

"Sully, this could be Mitchum's doing. He set up Nealy to fail in retrieving that drive. He knew where it was really located. And I don't trust him not to have set us up here too."

A splash sounded, and all three of them jerked. Nealy let out a sharp cry, and Linc's arms were around her before she clamped it off.

"There goes our ship's captain. They —"

"Jumped ship," Sully finished for Linc. "Get the fuck outta there. I think it might be rigged to blow."

Linc looked down into Nealy's eyes. "Don't ever trust anyone but yourself, me or one of these guys from Ranger Ops again. Got it?"

"Loud and clear," she answered.

* * * * *

Nealy had only ever seen Linc freaking out once before. And she'd hoped never to see it again.

But the man was standing with hands braced against the ship's hull as if he could break through it just by sheer brute strength. His head was hanging between his shoulders, and when she approached him, she heard him breathing hard, just as he'd been that day he called her to come to him.

"Linc." She laid a hand on his back, prepared to duck if he was out of his head and struck at her.

He was coherent.

Thank God.

"I need to breathe," he said faintly.

"Go find a paper bag," Lennon said, pulling open crate after crate and looking inside for some answer to their situation. Every crate was filled to the top with weapons that were meant to cross the border. Somehow, the men had been tipped off and abandoned ship—literally.

Another crate top crashed to the floor, and Lennon walked over it to get to the next.

Nealy racked her brain. They were below deck, with not so much as a porthole to break through and swim out. If they even could before Gulf waters rushed in.

They couldn't break through the sealed passage to the above deck either—both Lennon and Linc had tried to kick it in to no avail.

Suddenly, Linc spun to face her. When he grabbed her by the upper arms, she bit back a gasp of surprise. His eyes burned down into hers, illuminated by the headlamp he wore.

"I can't lose you," he rasped.

"We'll figure something out, Linc."

He wasn't paying attention to her, because was staring at his twin. "If we both die, Momma will be devastated. One of us has to make it out of here alive."

"We're both making it out alive. Now cut the bullshit. You're not locked inside a crate, man. Grab your balls and find us a way out like the brother I've looked up to my entire life."

Nealy's eyes flooded with tears, and she blinked rapidly to dispel them before they fell. There was no room for theatrics in this moment—it was life or death. She was pretty sure the people who'd locked them inside the hull were not going to let them peacefully drift out into the Gulf only to be rescued by the Coast Guard later.

They weren't going to lose all those guns for nothing. Millions of dollars' worth.

She cradled Linc's face. "We can do this. We just need to find a way out and off this ship."

"Right." He moved away from her and began scoping out every inch of the walls, running his hands over some spots as if searching for weak spots to punch through. Lennon did the same, and they met up in the middle.

They looked at each other.

"You know what you gotta do, Linc," Lennon grated out.

He fell away from the wall, taking a few steps back. Swinging his gaze to Nealy, she saw the determination cutting across his rugged face.

"I can get us outta here." He reached into his pack and yanked out a handful of items. One glance at them and Nealy put two and two together.

"Trust me," he said.

She nodded. "I do. And I love you, Linc."

He grinned, and seeing the joy cross his face made her fall in love with him even deeper. "Love you too, babe. I hope you're ready to barbecue some illegal weapons."

"At this point, I'm ready to barbecue my director if he's the one responsible for this."

His eyes darkened. "I'll be right there to hand you the tongs."

Chapter Twelve

Nealy's fingers were still cramped from pressing them so tightly over her ears.

Her fiancé sure knew how to get out of a tight jam — by way of a little firepower and a fuse.

Her head still rang from the explosion, and she barely remembered being tossed out of the hull and onto the above deck, that had been splintered into nothing. Or how she'd managed to crawl to a safer spot and leap into the dark waters.

She did, however, recall vividly when the sure hands of one of the Ranger Ops team had pulled her into the safety of a boat. And when Linc had landed behind her and pulled her into his arms.

Still unable to stop the shaking caused by the rush of adrenaline, she turned to look at the ship they'd just escaped.

Another explosion rocked it, and Linc shielded her with his big shoulders. She fought to get her head up and watch as the entire craft burst into flames and a second reverberation rocked it.

When it tipped onto its side and began to sink, dowsing some of the flames and creating a thick black cloud rolling through the air, she gasped.

"This is all so crazy," she said, not realizing she'd spoken aloud until Linc looked at her.

"Looks like you got out of there just in time," Sully said with a shake of his head.

Shaw punched Lennon in the shoulder. "Good thing you've got a talented bomb maker for a brother, man."

"No shit. I would have been crispy." He stared at the wreckage, orange flames reflecting in his eyes.

Nealy found Linc's hand on her waist and meshed their fingers, needing to feel closer to him as all this rolled over her.

The more she thought about Mark Mitchum, the more she knew he was giving her directives that were putting her on the line. Setting her up to fail at the very least — sending her to a grave at the worst. Either way, she'd been endangered by his commands.

No wonder Linc had wanted so much revenge on the men who'd held him prisoner. There wasn't a balm to soothe over that fury.

The fight wasn't over, though. They'd sunk over several million dollars' worth of weapons to the bottom of the Gulf, but there were still men to fight. More guns to be brought in. If she knew Linc, and she thought she did pretty well, he wasn't about to stop until every man in Operation X was imprisoned or in a body bag.

But she would fight alongside him every step of the way.

He was holding her so protectively, locked against his chest so she could barely move a muscle. She realized he'd fight her to keep her out of it. But that wasn't her, and he knew that too.

They'd just have to plow on until they came out on top. Even though they hadn't gotten the guys behind the crime, they had stopped those illegal arms from making their way into the hands of the population that would in turn kill innocent human beings.

It wasn't all a failure.

It was only a step toward the end result. Like her relationship with Linc.

They'd begun as enemies, become lovers and had plenty of ups and downs on the road here. Now, she relaxed in his hold and let him take over the duty of protecting her while she watched over his emotional wellbeing.

He seemed fine after creating that bomb, though, not affected at all, and now he was joking and ribbing Lennon about how he shouldn't have skipped leg day and been able to kick the door off the hatch.

Which led to Lennon bringing up a bunch of times when he bested Linc as kids. By the time they got off the water, her nerves had calmed a bit.

But as soon as the shouts sounded in her ear — and coming from behind her — she was back in the fight with the assholes who had sailed in under stealth of the night and managed to get their boats ashore.

Linc grabbed her and spun her around to face the fight head-on.

It was how she knew he trusted her as much as she trusted him.

She raised her weapon and took aim.

* * * * *

"What the hell just happened?" Sully rubbed a hand over his jaw and stared at the shoreline, and Linc moved up next to him to stare at the fucking hell they'd rained down on Operation X.

"Well, I'm not going to say we wiped the fuckers out, but we gave it a hell of a run this time," Linc said.

As Ranger Ops had engaged them in an all-out battle, their backup had moved in from both sides, Team Rou and Knight Ops providing the cover they needed to obliterate the dozens of small vessels that had suddenly appeared out of nowhere, manned with machine guns. They'd sprayed enough bullets over the shore that Linc swore he'd traveled back in time and landed on Omaha Beach in World War II.

A trickle of blood ran down his cheek, and he swiped it away. Sully looked at him. "Go get yourself taken care of."

Linc gripped Sully's shoulder. "You all right, man?"

"Fucking lucky to be alive. If Nevaeh knew about this, she'd never let me walk out the front door again."

Linc's lips tipped into a humorless smile. "Then you'd have to use the back door. And Sully... I don't recommend telling her the details."

"You can't exactly do that with your ATF agent, can you?" Sully and Linc turned to look at Nealy standing with Lennon, head bowed with either fatigue or because she was shattered by the things she'd seen and done. Linc still had to find out, but he was damn afraid of the control he'd given up so she could prove herself.

And that director of hers... Linc would bet his dominant hand that the man was ass-deep in Operation X, and she'd struck on something that would link him to the illegal smuggling.

He'd tried to throw her off with the flash drive, had sent her in with the wrong information so she failed, but Linc's gut instincts had guided him to retrieve the drive anyway. So when Nealy had returned to DC and placed it into her director's hands, he'd attempted to sweet-talk her with a promotion in order to throw her off his stench.

Then her director had sent her to stop the ship coming into port.

Which they knew had all been a trap.

Only they'd come out on top.

Since Nealy knew too much—and her director was well aware of it—she was even more of a target. At least until Linc personally escorted her back to Washington and personally fucked the man up enough with a warning to stay away from her.

"Go on," Sully said, seeing Linc staring at his fiancée.

As he crossed the ground that was littered with fallen bodies, she looked up at him. From here, he could see the tough-girl persona she claimed whenever she worked. But he knew underneath that callused skin was a woman he could unravel bit by delicious bit.

Lennon gave him a nod at his approach. "I'll hand her over to you."

Nealy dragged in a breath. "I don't need handed over or watched over, for that matter."

Linc grinned at his twin. "Now look what you've started."

"Have fun with that." Lennon moved away to the group of Knight Ops huddled together, talking and celebrating living through yet another day.

Nealy still had her mouth open, prepared to spit bullets at him, but he caught her by the hand and drew her away. When he found a spindly tree, he sank to the ground and leaned his back against it.

She stared down at him.

"C'mere," he said.

She glanced around.

"Nobody cares about us. C'mere," he said again, softer this time.

Her posture relaxed, and she settled beside him. He didn't hesitate to pull her across his lap and wrap his arms around her. When he bowed his nose into her hair and inhaled deeply, she gave a shiver and slipped her arms around his neck.

"Thank God nothing happened to you," he groaned out.

"Or you. Are you all right? After being trapped again and creating another bomb—"

He kissed her into silence. The gentle caress of mouth on mouth had his cock hardening immediately, and she wiggled over it.

They shared a moan.

When he withdrew, he stared into her eyes. Up close, they lit with desire but he read her well enough to see the worry there as well.

"I'm fine. Promise," he said.

She nodded and snuggled closer, tucking her head against his shoulder. He cupped her nape and held her there, just taking in the moment of respite before they fought yet another battle. Though the next wouldn't involve ammunition and his skill set with a tactical weapon, he did intend to make her job safer for her.

"You know we have to go back to DC, right?" he asked.

She moved back to look at him. "We?"

He nodded. "I won't let you go alone. We both know what the hell went down and who was behind it all."

With a sigh, she said, "I do. I was just hoping you wouldn't try to get involved."

"I've got your six—forever. And you need my word as a way to nail the bastard."

"My guess is he's been taking money from Operation X to *not* catch them."

"I'd say you're right."

He eyed her. "Looks like if he loses his job, you might be sitting at that desk sooner than you expected."

Studying his eyes, she gave a light shake of her head.

His brows pinched. "What is it?"

"Linc… I haven't discussed it with you yet, but I think I might transfer here. To one of the Texas offices. See what good I can do in this part of the country and toss my hat into the ring for a promotion nearby."

His heart pumped hard against his ribs. "Are you sure? The last thing I'd ask is for you to give up the job you want for me."

"It's not just for you. It's for us. Something about Texas changed me, you could say."

He grunted. "Well, it hasn't changed you enough."

She blinked in shock. "What? You don't think I belong here?"

"Didn't say that. But if you're stickin' around, you need to get your Texas talk down better. A Texan would never say you want to see what good you can do in 'this part of the country.'"

Confusion wrinkled her brow as she stared at him.

He smoothed a fingertip over her forehead. "They'd say 'this neck o' the woods,' babe. You'll just have to listen and learn, I guess. Hopefully in time, you'll be a Texas girl."

She narrowed her eyes at him, and he chuckled, drawing her tighter into his embrace.

"You have some things to teach me." Her voice hitched with a wobble of desire — he heard it loud and clear.

Rocking his hips up into hers, he ground his erection against her ass. She let out a rasp of a moan and leaned in, her lips a breath from his and her eyes beginning to blur with desire.

"I can't wait to get out of here and be alone with you," she whispered.

He captured her plump lower lip and gave it a suck. "I bet I could find a nice row of hedges to hide behind."

* * * * *

When Nealy entered the ATF offices, she didn't take five steps inside the door before people were popping up from their cubicles throughout the room. A round of applause greeted her.

She stopped in her tracks, aware of Linc right behind her, taking this reception in.

"Is this normal?" he asked.

"Of course. It's how they always greet me." She tossed a grin over her shoulder and began to move through the people, hearing congratulations so many times she lost count.

Her mind whirled about what was to come. As soon as she stepped into Mitchum's office and faced the man eye to eye, what would he have to say for himself?

She'd played scenarios over and over during the flight from Texas. And she could only guess at how Mark would attempt to throw her off his trail and twist things to make her seem incompetent or worse, hormonal.

Linc rested a hand on the small of her back. "You're tense. Don't let your thoughts get away with you. You can do this."

"Don't talk please. Don't try to back me up in there."

She'd said it half a dozen times during the flight, and he'd given his word that this was her show and she was the one running it. He was just here as a bodyguard.

Drawing a deep breath, she nodded. "Let's go."

She led the way to the acting deputy director's office. When she opened the door, she was stunned to see not Mark in one of his new suits—probably purchased with dirty money—but Chief of Staff Holden.

He offered her a big smile as she entered and looked to Linc. "Close the door, Alexander." He extended a hand to her and then Linc. "You must be Reed."

"Yes, sir."

"I hear our thanks are in order. We've been on the trail of these guys for months and without your team, we never could have stopped them."

Linc nodded and shook his hand. "You're welcome. But we couldn't have located them without Agent Alexander."

The man's eyes gleamed. "Let's not pretend there isn't more between you. I hear congratulations are in order." He smiled into her eyes.

She felt a flush climbing her cheeks, both with the pleasure of Linc giving her credit but because she hadn't had a chance to actually tell people the news about her engagement, yet her chief of staff knew.

Who else did? Heck, she hadn't even told her parents yet, and they'd kill her if they heard before she told them.

There was another question pressing on Nealy's mind.

"Sir... where is Mitchum?"

"We have some things to discuss, Alexander. Please sit." He gestured to the chairs, and she sank to one before Linc followed. She could feel the tension rolling off her fiancé. Since he had such a sixth sense about things, she couldn't help but feel edgy too.

Holden leaned back in the chair and eyed them both. "We have some big accusations thrown your way, agent."

She schooled her expression into that of calm. Or what she hoped passed for it. "I'd like the chance to defend those accusations, sir."

He nodded. Linc crossed one leg over the other, giving the impression he was cool and relaxed, but she knew by the set of his shoulders that was far from the truth. She had to do her best to defuse the situation before her lover took it upon himself to kick someone's ass on her behalf.

"Several things have been documented. First being that you viewed classified information on that flash drive."

Her brows shot up in surprise. "I was told to retrieve the drive, sir. Not research whatever data is on it."

Linc shifted, dropping his other boot to the floor with a thud. "I think the bigger question—" he began.

She placed a hand on his knee to stop him from speaking and looked up at her superior. "Linc's right, the bigger question is why I was told the drive was in one spot when it was in another."

"And how did you come to find it?" Holden asked.

"Linc discovered a difference in the wall, as if a panel had been cut out and papered over."

"Mistakes happen all the time, intel is fumbled. The fact that you did not have the right coordinates doesn't mean foul play," Holden said.

She nodded. "It was only one thing that tipped me off. The other..." she met Holden's eyes, "is that we didn't tell anybody where we actually found the drive, and yet Mitchum told me he knew it was in a different place."

Holden's lips tightened as he processed this. If he had something further to say, he was saving it. "There are other reports." He lifted some papers.

"May I see them?" she asked, reaching out.

He handed her the sheets, and she skimmed the text.

Linc was staring at her—she felt his heavy gaze boring into her, trying to read her. Later, he would hear her vent, that was certain. What she read had her seeing red and every shade of purple anger that existed.

She set the pages on the desk, but before Holden could take them, Linc snatched them up. She should wrench them from him, keep him from reading what they said about her.

But it was too late.

He wadded them up in his fist like they were tissue paper and dropped the ball on the floor. "This is total bullshit," Linc said.

"I think what he means to say is that if you look closely, you'll see the person who filed these was Mitchum. I have reason to believe he's been gunning for me all along. And that he is directly working with Operation X, perhaps accepting bribe money in order to turn a blind eye to what they're doing. When that failed, he provided wrong information, directed agents and the Ranger Ops away from them so they were not caught."

Holden looked at her for a long moment. "I had to know," he said.

Confusion hit her. "Sir?"

"I had to know if you were in on it with Mitchum. He's been stripped of his badge, his position and will likely see jail time for his role in Operation X. But he pointed the finger at you, said you were in on it as well."

Linc shot to his feet, the sheer power in his muscles seeming to thrum in the small office space. He slammed a fist onto the desk, causing Holden to jump in his seat and bringing Nealy to her feet.

"Linc, it's all right. Holden isn't accusing me. He's just said that he had to know if I was responsible. He's presented all this to us in order to see my reaction or catch me in a lie." She rested a hand on

Linc's shoulder in hope it was enough to keep him from going for the chief of staff's throat. She looked into Holden's eyes. "I will swear before any judge in this country that I had no knowledge of treason or treachery, other than my suspicions about Acting Deputy Director Mitchum."

"He doesn't bear those titles any longer," Holden said. "In fact," he tossed a look at Linc as if afraid of what he'd do at his next words, "the office is open and you *were* next in line for a promotion, Alexander."

* * * * *

"You had something to do with that," she tossed over her shoulder at Linc as she strode as fast as she could toward the elevators.

"Hell I did. That was all you, babe. He said himself you were next in line for a promotion. And why would he listen to a word I said? You saw how much the guy likes me — he looked ready to climb the office walls to escape me." He caught up to her by the elevators. She jabbed a button, and when the door didn't immediately open, she stabbed it repeatedly.

Linc caught her elbow and turned her to him, gently, slowly. She came, facing him but refusing to do more than stare at his chest.

Which she could do later — when he stripped them both and took her in a wild afternoon of passion that would lead to an evening and end in an all-nighter.

He was going to fuck his girl, and good too.

"Babe," he said quietly.

She pushed out a sigh through her nose. "I know you didn't really have anything to do with the promotion, Linc. Holden respects you, though. He'd take your word."

"Well, he should, but I think that respect is born of fear. Anyway, you turned it down. Why did you do that?"

"You know why." She lifted her eyes to his. Just then, the elevator door opened, and luckily nobody else was inside.

She followed him in, and they stood there a moment in silence before the doors shut.

Linc made his move.

Jamming his thumb into the emergency stop button, bringing the unit to a jerking halt, he lifted Nealy in his arms and crushed her against the wall with his lips over hers.

She cried out, and he devoured the sound as he fumbled over the buttons of her blouse and went to work on her pants. She ripped off his shirt and made a mewling sound of despair when she struggled with his belt.

He whipped it open for her, offering her a grin. "This time, the lights are on."

"Good. I need to watch your big cock sink into me." She kicked out of her clothes and fell into his arms. He lifted her, angled against the wall with his hands under her round ass as he sank his cock deep in one swift, slippery glide.

They went still for a second, gazes locked, and began to move.

His balls swung forward to brush her body with each churn of his hips. Under his lips, every single freckle raised into a goose bump to meet his kiss. He pressed kisses down her throat and snaked his tongue lower, over her nipple.

It beaded on his tongue, and she cried out, yanking him down by the nape to get closer as he sucked and pulled at her bud with his lips, teeth and tongue. Need was burning up from the base of his spine.

"It's only been about twenty-four hours since I had you, and I can't get enough," he rasped.

"What does that mean for our married life?" She dug the blunt points of her nails into his shoulders. He threw his head back on the harsh pleasure she gave as good as she got.

He pierced her in his gaze and shoved his cock deep into her pussy again. "It means we have some negotiating to do."

"Lemme hear it," she grated out, her words ending on a whimper as he reached a spot she liked.

"We do this at least once a day," he murmured against her lips, the throb increasing in his core.

"Only once? And does that mean we have to install an elevator in your apartment?"

He laughed, burrowing his face against her neck as he rocked with pleasure and total joy at having her in his life.

"More than once."

"As many times as we want." She sank her teeth into his earlobe and began to pulsate around him. Her inner muscles a flutter that soon became a tight clenching he couldn't resist.

"I'm coming!" she gasped out.

He tucked her close as she shuddered and his own orgasm hit with a force that stole his breath.

After the last stream of cum soaked her insides, he caught her gaze. "We at least need a wedding reception venue with at least one elevator."

"To consummate our marriage." She laughed, the throaty sound gripping him all over again.

Drawing out of her, he let her slip down until her feet touched the floor. This time, as they dressed, she gawked at his body and didn't try to cover herself like the first time they'd done it in an elevator.

He reached for her, and she wrapped her arms around him. He couldn't resist when she turned her head up for him to kiss her. The long, soft meshing of mouths drew the warmth of love into the moment, not that it had ever been missing.

She eyed the panel of buttons on the wall. "You want to do the honors of starting this thing, or should I?"

"I'll let you do the honor. Since it might be your last time in DC and you'll be a real Texas girl."

A gleam came into her eyes. "I'm ready and rarin' to go. Is that saying Texas enough for you?"

He laughed, and she restarted the elevator. When they reached the ground floor, she took him by the hand and tangled their fingers. Outside the door, he whirled her to him and kissed her.

"This is the start of our new life," she whispered, cupping his jaw.

He rested his forehead against hers, staring into her eyes. "Let's hop a flight and get to it."

Epilogue

Nealy looked around the crowded bowling alley, shocked that these big Ranger Ops dudes who could level a threat in seconds, were into such a weenie sport.

With Linc's hand on her back, he maneuvered her through the line of people renting shoes and on to the place where they could buy drinks.

"You ever bowled before?" He slanted a look at her.

"Once at a sixth grade birthday party. I wasn't any good."

He chuckled and stepped up to the bar. "Two drafts," he told the worker.

Nealy twisted to look at the lanes and people high-fiving someone who'd just bowled a strike. Then her gaze landed on two pretty females carrying trays of nachos with cheese and throwing looks at another group of men across the room.

They put their heads together and giggled at whatever was spoken between them, but following their stares, Nealy could guess it was about the hunky Ranger Ops taking up two lanes against the wall.

"You see the guys, babe? I'll carry the beers."

"I see them." She couldn't help but be more stunned to see how seriously the team was taking their game. When they approached, Lennon and Jess were involved in an argument, battling with words instead of fists, but she wouldn't be surprised if it came down to that. Each was as red-faced and angry as the other.

Linc set down the beers with a sigh. "Gotta make some peace here." He sidled over to the pair and stepped up between them.

His twin ducked around him and walked up to Jess. The other man looked as if he was about to roll up his sleeves and let Lennon have it.

"Hey, hey. It's just a game, guys."

"It's not a game. It's a woman," Cav spoke up from the sidelines, sounding overly cheerful at his friends' reason for arguing.

"She was with me last night," Jess was saying.

"Well, she was with me the night before that," Lennon spat.

"Which shows what she thought of your skills in bed." Jess laughed, and Shaw and Sully just shook their heads.

Nealy stood there a moment, engaged in watching, but a beautiful woman caught her eye.

"You must be Nealy," she said, brushing her dark hair over her shoulder.

Nealy nodded. "And you're... Sully's wife?"

She nodded. "Nevaeh. This is Atalee, Shaw's fiancée. Come sit with us—we have a better view of the fight from here, plus we have pretzels."

Nealy followed them—she wasn't giving up the offer of pretzels to go with her beer.

A second later, Jess and Lennon stepped around Linc and raised their hands. Nealy sucked in a breath, holding it as she looked on. But the guys just threw their arms around each other and clapped each other's back.

"Guess it's over," Atalee said with a grin.

Shaw came over to brush his lips across hers. "You're up, baby doll."

She groaned. "I suck so much." She threw a look at Nealy. "I'm warning you that if you're on this team, we won't win."

Nealy shrugged, really not caring one whit about bowling. But she couldn't deny the camaraderie was off the charts. She'd never seen the guys so relaxed. She could understand why the Pins 'n Sins was their hangout. They could let go and blow off steam, which was exactly what they needed with the stress they all endured.

She hoped to acclimate to a different kind of stress now that she'd just been transferred to the local ATF office and given her first glimpse at her workload. There was a lot of weapons and drug trafficking in this part of the country, and she looked forward to doing her part to stop it. Plus, she could go home every night to Linc's place. Even if he was out on some mission, she could still breathe his scent on the pillow beside her and feel shrouded by his love.

"Have you set a date yet?" Nevaeh asked after bowling her turn.

She shook her head. "We're just getting settled into life first. Neither of us are in any hurry."

"That's what I thought about Shaw too, and he wants to fix a date as soon as possible. He's even mentioned eloping to Vegas!" Atalee shook her head, gazing at the back of her handsome fiancé as he sipped his beer and BS'd with the guys.

At that moment, Linc moved in and pressed a kiss to Nealy's neck behind her ear. She curled her hand up around his jaw, enjoying the tingles he sent through her entire body at his caress.

"You're up next, babe," he whispered, taking her earlobe between his teeth and tugging.

She stifled a gasp and twisted her head toward him.

"Don't be surprised if I'm not pressuring you to take off for Vegas too very soon. I hear they have some very nice elevators in that town."

She giggled. "We'll be doing our wedding the traditional way, with all our family around us. And friends too." She looked at the group there, who were quickly becoming not only her friends but a new type of family.

He took her by the hand and hauled her up to her feet. "Let's prove to everyone that you can carry your weight on this team, babe. We need you to bowl a strike to get us back on track."

She groaned and shot looks at the women. "Oh no. I hope you're all prepared for disappointment."

"Let me show you how it's done." Linc positioned the ball in her hands and then stepped up behind her to show her the proper form. All he managed to do was turn her on with his erection pressed into her backside and his warm breath tickling across her ear.

When she bowled straight down the middle, knocking down nine of the ten pens, a cheer went up from all. Nealy turned into Linc's arms, and he grinned. "Full of surprises, aren't you, babe?"

She cocked a brow at him. "Don't ever underestimate me, Reed."

He watched her walk away a moment before catching her at the booth where they all sat. "I know exactly what you're capable of, Alexander."

She angled her head. "What's that?"

"You're capable of turning me on more than anything in the world, and of driving me completely crazy at the same time."

"It's what brought us together," she said.

"And what will keep us together." His eyes gleamed as he leaned in for a kiss.

THE END

Em Petrova

Em Petrova was raised by hippies in the wilds of Pennsylvania but told her parents at the age of four she wanted to be a gypsy when she grew up. She has a soft spot for babies, puppies and 90s Grunge music and believes in Bigfoot and aliens. She started writing at the age of twelve and prides herself on making her characters larger than life and her sex scenes hotter than hot.

She burst into the world of publishing in 2010 after having five beautiful bambinos and figuring they were old enough to get their own snacks while she pounds away at the keys. In her not-so-spare time, she is fur-mommy to a Labradoodle named Daisy Hasselhoff and works as editor with USA Today and New York Times bestselling authors.

Find Em Petrova at empetrova.com

Other Titles by Em Petrova

Ranger Ops
AT CLOSE RANGE
WITHIN RANGE
POINT BLANK RANGE

Knight Ops Series
ALL KNIGHTER
HEAT OF THE KNIGHT
HOT LOUISIANA KNIGHT
AFTER MIDKNIGHT
KNIGHT SHIFT
ANGEL OF THE KNIGHT
O CHRISTMAS KNIGHT

Wild West Series
SOMETHING ABOUT A LAWMAN
SOMETHING ABOUT A SHERIFF
SOMETHING ABOUT A BOUNTY HUNTER
SOMETHING ABOUT A MOUNTAIN MAN

Operation Cowboy Series
KICKIN' UP DUST
SPURS AND SURRENDER

The Boot Knockers Ranch Series
PUSHIN' BUTTONS
BODY LANGUAGE
REINING MEN
ROPIN' HEARTS
ROPE BURN
COWBOY NOT INCLUDED

LIPSTICK 'N LEAD

The Dalton Boys
COWBOY CRAZY Hank's story
COWBOY BARGAIN Cash's story
COWBOY CRUSHIN' Witt's story
COWBOY SECRET Beck's story
COWBOY RUSH Kade's Story
COWBOY MISTLETOE a Christmas novella
COWBOY FLIRTATION Ford's story
COWBOY TEMPTATION Easton's story
COWBOY SURPRISE Justus's story
COWGIRL DREAMER Gracie's story

Single Titles and Boxes
STRANDED AND STRADDLED
LASSO MY HEART
SINFUL HEARTS
BLOWN DOWN
FALLEN
FEVERED HEARTS
WRONG SIDE OF LOVE

Club Ties Series
LOVE TIES
HEART TIES

MARKED AS HIS
SOUL TIES
ACE'S WILD

Firehouse 5 Series
ONE FIERY NIGHT
CONTROLLED BURN
SMOLDERING HEARTS

The Quick and the Hot Series
DALLAS NIGHTS
SLICK RIDER
SPURRED ON

EM PETROVA
WWW.EMPETROVA.COM

Made in United States
Troutdale, OR
05/05/2024

19642758R00136